JACKRABBIT
SMILE

BOOKS BY JOE R. LANSDALE

THE HAP AND LEONARD NOVELS

Savage Season
Mucho Mojo
The Two-Bear Mambo
Bad Chili
Rumble Tumble
Captains Outrageous
Vanilla Ride
Devil Red
Honky Tonk Samurai
Rusty Puppy
Jackrabbit Smile

OTHER NOVELS

The Magic Wagon
The Drive-In
The Nightrunners
Cold in July
The Boar
Waltz of Shadows
The Bottoms
A Fine Dark Line
Sunset and Sawdust
Lost Echoes
Leather Maiden
All the Earth, Thrown to the Sky
Edge of Dark Water
The Thicket
Paradise Sky

SELECTED SHORT-STORY COLLECTIONS

By Bizarre Hands
Sanctified and Chicken-Fried
The Best of Joe R. Lansdale

JACKRABBIT
SMILE

JOE R.
LANSDALE

MULHOLLAND BOOKS

Little, Brown and Company

New York Boston London

Mulholland Books / Little, Brown and Company
Hachette Book Group
1290 Avenue of the Americas, New York, NY 10104
mulhollandbooks.com

First Edition: March 2018

Mulholland Books is an imprint of Little, Brown and Company, a division of Hachette Book Group, Inc. The Mulholland Books name and logo are trademarks of Hachette Book Group, Inc.

The publisher is not responsible for websites (or their content) that are not owned by the publisher.

The Hachette Speakers Bureau provides a wide range of authors for speaking events. To find out more, go to hachettespeakersbureau.com or call (866) 376-6591.

ISBN 978-0-316-31158-8
Library of Congress Control Number: 2018930642

10 9 8 7 6 5 4 3 2 1

LSC-C

Printed in the United States of America

To the memory of friend, fine actor, photographer,
artist, and filmmaker Bill Paxton, who was taken
way too soon

It is wiser to find out than to suppose.

> —Mark Twain

Question with boldness even the existence of a god; because, if there be one, he must more approve the homage of reason, than that of blindfolded fear.

> —Thomas Jefferson

1

Even when I'm doing something enjoyable, it seems death and destruction lurk nearby. I might not recognize those dual demons right away, but they're out there.

They might arrive in a pickup truck, and those in it may seem at first like a lot of people I might see. Just folks going about their business.

But they may be carriers of a repulsive kind of disease, and there are many symptoms. Hate and prejudice, ignorance and a profound pride in what they don't know. They are those who go with their gut, which is about as accurate as throwing chicken bones or reading signs in frog entrails.

I don't know they're coming until they're there, and even then, I might not understand exactly what has walked into my life. I may think, considering my experience, that I'll know right away if something is going to go dark and wet, but I still get fooled, and their kind of disease can have a ripple effect; it's not just their viewpoint, it's how their viewpoint affects others—they spread their germs without even being aware of it.

• • •

I was in the side yard with Brett, enjoying our Saturday, and a fine April afternoon, cooking up burgers, bratwurst, and weenies on the grill. Their aroma in the air was thick enough, if you smacked your lips you could taste them.

We were celebrating. Three hours before, me and Brett had gotten married by the LaBorde justice of the peace. No Bible, no preacher, just the law. Me and her had talked about pulling that trigger for some years, and finally we had gone and done it. I couldn't have been happier.

When we got married we had a small crowd there at the JP's office, close friends and a few strays we had taken in, and they were coming over in a little while to enjoy our wedding picnic. We had a long folding-leg table laid out with paper plates and cups, and an ice chest with a bag of ice in it. We had folding chairs stacked on the ground, ready for use.

I was scraping a burger off the grill, flipping it.

"I thought we might go to Paris for a honeymoon," Brett said, "but then I got to thinking about a cookout in the yard and nixed it."

"Yeah. French cooking can kiss my ass, baby. I'm doing burgers and dogs."

"Don't burn them this time," Brett said.

"Nope. I'm on it. And you know what, everything goes well, we can play horseshoes after lunch, and later tonight you can play with my ass."

"Oh, you charmer."

"That's right, baby. Stick with me and you'll be farting through silk."

A white pickup coasted to the curb in front of our house and parked next to the oak tree that grew near the street. It wasn't a truck that belonged to one of our guests. It wasn't a truck that belonged to anybody I knew.

The tires on the truck were so high that when the door opened, the driver, a thin, thirtyish man with wiry muscles and sandy-blond hair, practically had to dangle himself down to the curb. On the other side a woman worked her way out of the passenger seat and came around the front of the truck. She had lowered some kind of step stool to make her exit. I caught a glimpse of it from under the truck. Both of them probably had nosebleeds from sitting so high.

They started across the yard. It made me a little nervous, especially when I saw the T-shirt the man was wearing. It was white with blue lettering on the front that read WHITE IS RIGHT. Not one of my sentiments, even though my skin is as pale as milk when it isn't tanned or sunburned.

The young man had on black jeans and lace-up boots and so many tattoos visible on his arms and neck that, from a distance, I thought he was wearing long sleeves. Close up I could see more tattoos through the thin fabric of his T-shirt. I assumed he might have others in places less interesting to see, and a box of stick-on tattoos at home along with a pointed white hood for those special evenings out with the Klan. That may sound judgmental, but hey, that T-shirt told me a lot.

The woman was probably in her late fifties, garbed up in what I think of as traditional Pentecostal style, meaning her brown hair was in a bun so tall and wide she could have hidden an electric mixer under it, and she was wearing a blue-jean dress that fell almost to her ankles and was capped off by clunky black boots that looked one grade up from orthopedic shoes. She didn't have on any makeup, not even lipstick or eyeliner. From certain religious points of view, God and Jesus get all worked up about hairdos and makeup but couldn't seem to end a war anywhere or kill a disease. I thought maybe God had his priorities out of whack.

Those two looked so much like stereotypes it wouldn't have surprised me to discover they had venomous snakes in their pockets and could speak in tongues.

The man slowed and let the woman take the lead. She came right to me, stuck out her hand, and I shook it. She didn't offer it to Brett. The man didn't offer his hand to either of us. He stood there with his hands in his pockets. One eyelid spasmed from time to time, as if being periodically electrocuted. I could have sworn I saw one of his neck tattoos crawl under his shirt, but I suppose it was a shifting of the light.

Up close I could see some of the tattoos were professional and some were the sort you do yourself or get in prison, or perhaps a three-year-old with a carving knife and a bottle of ink had been hired to mark him up.

"You're the one's got that private detective agency, aren't you?" the woman said.

"She does," I said, nodding at Brett. "I work for her."

"Oh, I thought you owned it and had her and that . . . colored fellow working for you. What's he do there?"

"Eats cookies and drinks coffee, from what I can tell," I said.

"He works there, same as this man, who, by the way, is my husband."

I liked the way Brett said that. I felt like a big dog. I was so happy I wanted to wag my tail.

"You work for your wife?" the man said. It was like his mind had just snapped to attention.

"It's either that or she doesn't let me eat."

"Sometimes, when he's sassy or acting a little hysterical, I make him stand in the yard and hold a heavy rock over his head," Brett said.

The woman grinned a little, but the young man looked at me as if he were concerned I not only didn't wear the pants in the family but might have accidentally cooked my dick on the grill in place of a sausage.

"We looked you up in the phone book. Drove by your office a few times," the woman said. "We asked around about y'all, trying to decide."

"Decide what?" Brett said.

"We got this problem, and truth is, everyone else turned us down."

"Who's everyone else?" I said.

"The other private detective in town."

"There's another one?" I said.

"And all them over in Tyler and Longview too. Ain't none over in Marvel Creek, which is where we've got the problem, so there wasn't no one to ask there. Cops here can't do nothing. It's out of their jurisdiction."

"Thing is, we heard you had that nig...colored man working there," the young man said, "and that put us off some. At first we thought he just cleaned up the office."

5

I thought: Bless your little ignorant heart.

"Here's something might put you off even more," I said, and pointed.

Marvin Hanson's car pulled up at the curb, and he and Officer Carroll, as we always called Curt, got out.

Hanson was carrying a twelve-pack of diet sodas under his arm, and Officer Carroll had a twelve-pack of beer under his. The sodas were mostly for me, the beers were for some of the others.

From the backseat came the niece of Leonard's ex-boyfriend John. Her name was Felicity, and she was just out of her teens and had her hair in pigtails today, tied up on both sides with bright blue ribbons.

Finally, there was Reba, the little girl Leonard called the Four-Hundred-Year-Old Vampire Midget. Truth was, twelve years old or not, Reba could be a bitch. She had a mouth like a sailor's and a mind as sharp as a butcher's knife. I had to make sure she didn't get in the beer when no one was watching.

All of them except Officer Carroll were black as black could be, and you could see the man and the woman taking that in, the way soldiers might count their enemies' artillery mounted on a hill. Officer Carroll was Leonard's boyfriend. I kind of figured same-sex relationships were probably on the pair's no-no list as well.

"What's all them colored people showing up for?" the young man said. The way he said that, you could tell he didn't go out and about among those who held different beliefs than his own.

"We're filming a Tarzan movie after lunch," Brett said. "Need a lot of them colored folks for that. Cannibal scenes, you know."

"Yeah, I get to play Tarzan," I said.

"No. You get to be Tarzan's monkey," Brett said.

I made a soft chattering sound. I thought it sounded like a monkey, and a damn sexy monkey.

"By the way," I said, motioning to Marvin and Officer Carroll, "this gentleman is the police chief, and this white fellow works for him."

No hands were shook. Everyone merely looked at one another for a moment as if all fingers had been dipped in shit.

Marvin said, "We'll put these in the ice chest," and he and Officer Carroll went to do just that.

I heard the screen door slam and looked up to see Chance step out on the porch with a large bag of potato chips in either hand. She wasn't going to please them either. Physically, she was not only made up of whatever I was made up of, but she had her mother's coloring, her dark skin, fine American Indian and Hispanic features, black hair tied back in a ponytail long enough to use for a lariat. She was beautiful.

Right behind her came Leonard, in charge of a box of vanilla cookies, his black face split with a bright white smile.

I watched the young man fold his arms across his chest, obscuring the writing on his shirt.

Everyone came over and wished us congratulations again— everyone except our surprise guests, of course.

It was then a second wave of guests arrived. Our friend Manuela Martinez got out of her car carrying a large paper bag. She was looking fine and petite in tight jeans and an equally tight orange top, her black hair cut to the shoulders; the white scar that ran from below her left ear to the tip of her chin gave her near-model features a kind of rugged class. I watched her walk toward us. I watched very carefully.

Brett elbowed me. "Watch it, mister."

"Hey, what was that for?" I said.

"You know," she said.

On the other side of the car, Cason Statler got out. He too had a paper bag with something in it. We were going to have enough food to feed the proverbial army. I had introduced him to Manny, as we called Manuela, and since that time they had become as tight as superglue in a gnat's ass.

Cason was one of those guys that got better looking as he got older. White guy with thick, dark hair and a cock-of-the-walk stride, always in shape.

Brett said, "Now I got something to look at."

"Then we're even," I said.

"Not exactly," she said.

The woman and the man from the two-story pickup truck stood stiff, like trees growing in the yard. We had sidelined them. And realizing we were being dicks, even though I thought they deserved it, I said, "Look, you want to talk, we can. On the porch."

They pulled roots and went to the porch and sat down on the glider and waited for us.

Leonard walked up to me, said, "Who are those crackers?"

"Why, those are racists who are a little worried we might have a colored boy working for us."

"Ah, now, Massa Hap, you know I'm one of the good ones."

"Yes, but don't forget your place."

"You mean with my foot up your ass?" he said.

Chance listened to us and smiled. She carried the chips to the table. Me and Brett greeted everybody while Leonard went on over to the porch to make the honkies nervous. He smelled blood in the water.

I gave the spatula to Manny, said, "Don't let the food burn."

"I warn you," Manny said, "what I cook best are kitchens. I've burned down two of them."

"No worries," Brett said. "We're outdoors. If the meat starts to smoke, use the spatula and take them off the grill. If they catch fire, use the spatula to beat out the flames."

"Gotcha," Manny said.

2

Me and Brett went over to the porch. As we were walking up, I heard Leonard say, "And I had me four of them fat white women in that barn. Lined 'em up against the wall, said, 'Strip off and bend over and call me Daddy.' Whole thing only cost me three dollars, and they let me brand them with a hot tire iron for free."

"Ignore him," I said.

The woman and the young man looked as if they had just survived a home invasion. The man especially appeared confused, and maybe a little angry, and yet at the same time there was a hesitation. I think he was afraid to say anything directly to Leonard, fearing his mouth might be writing a check his ass couldn't cash.

All of us were on the porch now, our guests in the glider, me and Brett sitting on the steps, and Leonard leaning against the front door.

"Them two, the colored and the white man, they really law?" the white guy asked.

"Naw," Leonard said. "We just let Marvin wear a badge and the other one got a cop suit for Christmas. Only reason he isn't wearing it now is for fear of mustard stains."

That got a blank look, an expression those two did especially well.

I said, "Yes. They are the real deal. First things first. I sense a disturbance in the color barrier. If you have trouble with black people, brown people, highly attractive redheads like my wife, or exceptional people like myself, then there's no use in us talking."

"All except that part about Hap being exceptional is real," Leonard said.

The man looked at his mother. His eye was twitching a little more frequently now.

His mother said, "I guess we're okay."

"I don't know," the man said. "I'm not sure a colored is up to the job. So we need to know how much he'll be involved."

"As much as any of us will," Brett said.

"Though during the middle of the day, I might have to have me a nap," Leonard said.

The man and woman looked at each other, didn't speak, but when they turned back to us, the woman said, "All right, then. Beggars can't be choosers."

"That's the spirit," Leonard said. He was talking cool, but the anger was coming off him like a high fever.

Brett reached out and gently touched Leonard's arm. He calmed beneath her hand.

"Okay, tell us who you are, what you want," Brett said.

"My name is Judith Mulhaney. This is my son, Thomas. What we want is to hire you to find my missing daughter. His sister, Jackie."

"We called her Jackrabbit," Thomas said. "She has these big

front teeth. Looked good on her, though. That's how we got to calling her a jackrabbit, saying she had a jackrabbit smile."

"She's been gone from home five years," Judith said. "Be honest, I don't think she's alive. Not to say she's been dead for five years. She was alive during most of that time, we know that. People saw her, but we didn't, just heard how she was doing here and there. Thought eventually, things would work out, that she'd come back to see us, but in the past few months, no one has seen her that we're aware of. Got to say we don't know many people over there well enough to be sure if we're getting the correct news. We kind of keep to ourselves. But I got a bad feeling. A mother knows."

"If anything was done to her," Thomas said, "I got an idea who might have done it."

"We want her back," Judith said, "be it flesh, or be it bones."

"All right," Brett said. "Before we know if we can be of any help, we need to hear the whole story. Need to know if you got money. Investigations don't come cheap."

"You get right to it, don't you?" Judith said.

"I do," Brett said. "You want us to do this, put us to work, you got to understand I don't like you or your son. You've insulted Leonard here several times and are too dense to know it or too insensitive to care. You've done everything but call him the N-word."

"I can say 'nigger,'" Leonard said. "It's okay I do. 'Nigger, nigger, nigger.'"

"Goddamn it, Leonard," Brett said.

"Just saying," Leonard said.

"That's what I don't get," Thomas said. "You can say it, but I can't."

"Oh, you can say it," Leonard said, "but say it with me standing here, next time you say it, it might be through a gap in your teeth. I say 'nigger,' we call it ironic, don't we, Hap?"

"Ironic," I said.

"You say it, and we knock your teeth out."

"It don't seem fair," Thomas said.

"It's on account of things having been so damn fair for us dark-skinned folks all these years. That too is irony, if you're wondering. And that doesn't mean something you do with starch and an ironing board."

"I know what 'irony' means," Thomas said. I didn't think he sounded all that convincing.

"Look here," I said. "Me and Brett, we're celebrating, and I don't want to deal with this. I'm sorry, but Jackie's been gone five years, she can wait a day. This is our day. Meet us at our office tomorrow at ten a.m., if you're serious. You know where the office is, I take it?"

Judith and Thomas both nodded in concert.

"And by the way. How did you find our house?" I said.

"Address is in the phone book," Thomas said.

"We looked up Brett Sawyer, like on the agency listing, and there's a house address for Brett Sawyer," Judith said. "We just drove over."

"Oh," I said.

So much for our Fortress of Solitude.

3

Me and Brett lay in bed breathing hard, our bodies covered in sweat. I was holding her in my arms and the air was beginning to cool. She reached over and grabbed the sheet and pulled it over us.

"Ah," I said, "you're blocking my view."

"You've seen enough for one night. My ass hurts."

"That was our first sex as a happily married couple," I said.

"Not to look a gift horse in the mouth, but it was a whole lot like the sex we had before we were married."

"This is true," I said. "But good, nonetheless."

"Absolutely. I'm glad we finally did it, Hap. Married, not had sex. Well, that came out wrong. I'm glad we did both. I don't know why being married matters, but it does. I didn't think it would. I knew you wanted to, and then I wanted to because you did, and now that we're married, I do feel different. I like it. Of course, I had a couple beers at lunch."

"It's a solid commitment, and I think it helps on our taxes."

"Married people break up all the time," she said.

"Not this time."

"Right answer," she said. "Do you think we were kind of mean to those people today?"

"I do. And they had it coming."

"Maybe we just fulfilled their idea of what liberal-minded folks are supposed to be like. Well, you're the most liberal-minded, and Leonard, he's not liberal, so maybe I don't know shit."

"Leonard was a real asshole," I said. "Talking about lining women up against the wall. He should have said men if he really wanted to get to them. Women aren't his attraction."

"I understand the sentiment," Brett said, and rubbed my thigh under the sheet.

"I don't know if I want to help those two," I said. "I really don't like them."

"It's not about their beliefs, Hap, it's about the missing girl."

"Jackrabbit."

"I bet she hated that name."

"Probably didn't use it with the general public," I said.

"Thinking it over," Brett said, "I think Leonard showed tremendous restraint."

"Yeah, couple years back he would have set their truck on fire with them in it."

"Think they'll show up at the office in the morning?"

"I don't know. But if you keep rubbing my thigh, I can tell you what will show up."

"That's kind of the idea," she said. "Question? You mind I'm keeping my last name, not taking yours?"

"Of course not. I'm keeping mine. I don't want to be Hap Sawyer any more than you want to be Brett Collins. I have thought about changing my name to Swinging Dick, though. Think that suits me better."

"Oh, baby. Name like that, wouldn't you need enough to swing, to give it meaning?"

"Oh, that hurt."

Brett laughed that throaty laugh she has and took hold of my head and pulled me to her and kissed me.

4

In the morning, we got up and had coffee and buttered toast, then showered together. It felt funny having the house all to ourselves again. First Leonard had moved in for a while, then he was gone, then Chance came in, and then she got an apartment and was out, then Reba the Four-Hundred-Year-Old Vampire Midget stayed with us for a couple of nightmarish weeks, then Reba moved in with Chance, who could stand her best, and then Buffy, the dog Leonard had rescued but who lived with us, moved in with Chance as well. Buffy and Reba had the least bit of luggage, unless you counted all that was packed up in their pasts. Mistreated girl, mistreated dog.

After showering, we ended up having sex on the couch, just because we could, then we got dressed, and Brett drove us to the office in her car. The bike shop under our office was opening up. I always tried to take a glance at the owner, a beautiful blond lady who wore shorts most of the time, even in cool weather, and in cold weather she wore yoga pants that didn't do her any harm either. I didn't see her this morning, but I looked anyway. I love my redheaded woman, but I won't lie: I enjoy examining the female form. I like to think it's the potential artist in me. But it's probably hormones. I think I got an extra share.

Leonard was already in the office making coffee and eating from a bag of vanilla cookies. There was a large watermelon on the desk next to a stack of moon pies and a can of malt liquor. On the wall, his fedora hung on a nail, and beside it, on another nail, was a straw cowboy hat about the size of a bird feeder. He wore hats from time to time, these and another one he kept at home, an actual deerstalker cap, like Sherlock Holmes in the movies, but he was going through a hatless period and had taken to shaving his head. I think this was due to his hair thinning.

As we came in, Leonard said, "And how are the newlyweds?"

"About like we were before we were newlyweds," Brett said. "Except, oh my God, the sex was amazing. We saw little stars."

"Really, we did," I said. "We bumped our heads on the headboard."

"I don't want to hear about it," Leonard said. "The idea of heterosexual sex always makes me queasy."

"Now that we've got that out of the way," I said, "why is there a watermelon, moon pies, and a can of malt liquor on the desk?"

"I was hoping, those two showed up, I would fit the stereotype. Just love jacking with them."

"Not today," Brett said. "Put that stuff out of sight. I thought about it all night. They may be assholes, but if they hire us, they're our assholes, so let's treat them like clients. We can dislike them on our off-hours."

"You're no fun," Leonard said, but he started moving the stuff off the desk and into the closet. He said, "I actually did bring all this stuff from home, except the malt liquor. That's Officer Carroll's. Had time, I'd have bought a bucket of chicken to go with this stuff."

"Just finish putting it away," Brett said. Then to me: "And you, mister. You can stop grinning. There's sweeping up needed around here."

"Yes, ma'am," I said.

I got the broom and dustpan and went at it, especially under the desk, where dirt was inclined to mound up from our shoes.

"Ha-ha," Leonard said, watching me sweep. "You missed a spot."

I finished up sweeping, checked the clock, saw it was a minute before ten.

Right then Brett said, "Here they are."

She was standing by the window looking out at the parking lot. Leonard and I went over to look out with her. The same truck on big high tires was there, and the side we could see was the passenger side this time, and when Judith opened the door, she pushed a button and a series of steps folded out of the truck and down to the ground. She came down them, hit another button, and they folded up. Smaller tires could have eliminated the steps and the money required for them, but I guess their version of Jesus liked white people to have plain hair and clothes and an expensive, big-ass, gas-guzzling truck.

Judith closed the door and started toward our office with her son, Thomas, who came around the front of the truck and joined her.

"I was hoping they wouldn't show up," Leonard said. "Hit by a car or something."

"That's not nice," Brett said.

"Like I don't know," Leonard said.

Brett sat down behind the desk, Leonard leaned against the wall, and I took a seat on the edge of the desk, near enough so I could bask in Brett's glow.

We listened to them climbing the stairs, and after a pause, they came in. The woman was dressed the same as yesterday, but Thomas had traded in his WHITE IS RIGHT T-shirt for a black one that had HARLEY-DAVIDSON written on it above the company's logo.

"Would y'all like some watermelon?" Leonard said. "I got one in the closet. I like to keep them around. I always got one at the ready. Moon pies too. Or maybe you'd like to wet your whistle with some malt liquor."

They looked at Leonard but didn't respond. Sometimes that's all you can do, ignore him. He's kind of like a dangerous wild animal; responses only encourage them.

Brett glared at him. Leonard gave them a little smile, like a farmer who had been caught with his finger in a duck's ass.

I offered them the client chairs, and they took their seats. When they were comfortable, Brett said, "Listen. We were rude to you yesterday. I don't apologize for why I was rude, but I apologize for being rude. We take your case on, you can be assured you'll get our best service."

"You won't just take our money," Thomas said.

"No," Brett said. "We won't. First, you have a photo of Jackie?"

Judith produced a couple from her purse and handed them to Brett. Brett looked at them, handed them to me. I had expected to see a girl with prominent teeth so extended she could eat an ear of corn through a split-rail fence, but Jackie was actually quite attractive, long, dark hair, the teeth even and white, but large. It made her kind of sexy-looking, I thought. She was probably in her early twenties in that shot, and it was obviously taken in a photo booth. The other was a picture of her and an older man, both leaning on a pickup truck. In that one she was younger, late teens, maybe, a little lost-looking, her face having yet to grow into her teeth. The guy was perhaps ten years older, or had lived a rugged life. He was big and dressed in camouflage pants and a white T-shirt. Guess a deer saw him from the belt down, he'd be invisible out there in the woods. There was about him a redneck air I always despise, a look on his face like a man that embraced ignorance as truth and lack of interest in education as a reward.

I gave the photos to Leonard. While he looked at them, Judith began to explain about Jackie's disappearance.

"Fellow that's with her," she said, "that's George Jeeter, over in Marvel Creek. He took up with her when she was sixteen. He's thirty in that picture. He'd be right on thirty-five or so now. Owns a junkyard. Jackie was always good with numbers, made good grades in school. She did George's books, or computer records, whatever it was. She wanted to be an accountant. George kicked her out, or she left him. Not clear on that, but they quit being together, we know that much."

"I'm presuming you went to Marvel Creek for a peek?" Brett said.

"Did," Thomas said. "Went over there and found Jeeter, but he claimed he hadn't seen her, not since he let her go. Said he didn't want to stay with her because she nagged him. I thought right then he'd done something to her."

"But you don't know that for a fact?" I said.

"No," Thomas said. "Guess I don't, but he's that kind of man.

He don't go to church none, even though he's got the right way of seeing things on certain issues."

"You mean he's a racist, like you two?" Leonard said.

"Segregationist," Thomas said. "I ain't got a thing against nig-gers—sorry. Habit."

"I bet," Leonard said, and the look on his face might have made Thomas pee himself a little.

Thomas rushed to doctor the wound. "Ain't got nothing against you or your kind, long as we all stay in our place, same as birds do. You don't see no mockingbird mating with a blue jay, now, do you?"

"People aren't birds," I said.

"Tommy, you are seriously stupid," Leonard said.

Thomas's response to this was "No one calls me Tommy."

"But they must call you stupid," Leonard said.

Thomas edged off his chair a little, but just a little. Leonard didn't blink. Tension in the room grew thick as cold molasses.

"Let's forget all that for now," Brett said. "Judith. Give us any-thing you think we should know. Leonard, tuck it back in, baby. We all know who's the man here. You're manly too, Hap."

"Thanks," I said. "I wasn't having any doubts."

"Well, I don't know how to say this," Judith said, "and I ain't proud of it, but now and again, when her and George would split up, 'cause they did that often, she'd run with colored boys."

"Was she a fast runner?" Leonard said.

"I don't mean like track," Judith said.

"I know what you meant," Leonard said.

Brett said, "Ground rules. We will all be polite. Especially you, Leonard."

"She ran with colored because she knew that would bother

George," Judith said. "Or that's what I think. She wasn't as particular as the rest of us. She liked life a little on the trashy side."

I heard Leonard sigh like air going out of a punctured tire. Brett shot him a look. He twisted his mouth as if to knot it and stayed quiet.

Brett turned her attention back to our potential clients.

"So, you're thinking it might not be George did her in but these colored boys, as you call them? And you, Thomas, you think it was George?"

"We don't know nothing for sure," Thomas said. "Did, we wouldn't need you people. But yeah, my guess is George did her in. I'd like to kill who did it myself, but I don't want to get cross with the law. Already done that. Spent a little time in Huntsville. Another strike, I'll be doing prison laundry for the rest of my life."

"You know the names of the black men she dated?" I asked.

"Only know of one, the main one, goes by the name Ace," Thomas said. "Me and Mom went asking around, and we didn't find out much but that. It wasn't like we were hanging with the same people she was hanging with."

"You mean the black people," Leonard said.

"Yeah, that's right," Thomas said. "On the other hand, George might have done something for his honor, and maybe that's all right, maybe I can understand that some, but still—"

"It's your sister," I said, finishing his thought.

"That's right," Thomas said. "Thing I want to know is if he done it. And for what reason. Hell, I've thought about killing her myself for breaking sacred bonds. Some things are about honor and blood."

"You mean she shouldn't have crossed the color line?" I said.

"That's right," Thomas said. "It's in the Bible. You don't do that.

I got a twenty-two at the house, and I might be inclined to use it on her. I sure thought about it."

"It's also in the Bible not to eat pork," I said, "but you look like a bacon-and-eggs kind of guy to me."

"It was okay for Jesus to eat what he wanted," Thomas said. "And I said I thought about it, but she was all right, except for not knowing where the boundary lines ought to be. Me and her had fun as kids. We got along good then."

I thought him saying how she was all right sounded about as sincere as a lion trying to talk an antelope into cuddling.

"They did have fun," Judith said. "They were little scamps."

"Tell you what," Brett said. "I'm going to give you a pen and a tablet, and I want you to write down any information you have about Jackie and people she might know, black or white, the connections they had with her. Close friends, relatives, you name it. Not just people you might think could have done something to her but even those you feel certain wouldn't do anything to her. Write it all down, and if you have a stray thought about this or that, something pertaining to Jackie, put that down too."

Brett opened the desk drawer, pulled out a couple of yellow-paper tablets and slid them across the desk, gave them a pen apiece.

They took the tablets and started writing. We all sat in silence while they did. The only sounds in the room were the ball-point pens scratching on paper.

When they finished, they slid the tablets and pens back. Brett picked up Judith's tablet, and I picked up Thomas's. I had a pang of sadness when I saw he'd misspelled every other word and couldn't write a sentence that was a complete thought. He had some ideas he wanted to express, and they were pretty much the same thing he had said before, about Jackie maybe being dishonorable for running with colored. He spelled "honor" as "oner." I felt sorry for him right then. I wished I had never said a harsh word to him or her. I felt like a bully, picking on a mentally deficient mark.

It was a feeling I knew would soon pass. Sometimes there are people who deserve to be treated like assholes. I know I've had it coming more than once.

"How about Jackie's father?" Brett asked. "What's his story?"

"Sebastian. His name's on there. I pretty much raised the kids alone," Judith said. "He went another way, lost his religion, joined the Presbyterians or some such."

"Also Christians," I said.

"Not according to the Bible," Judith said. It was as if she were trying to explain to us that red wasn't green. It was obvious to her.

"Tomayto, tomahto," Leonard said.

"The true word of the Lord will be known to those who wish to accept it," Judith said. "Presbyterians are infidels."

"Tomayto, tomahto," Leonard said again.

"So he doesn't have any connection to the children?" Brett said.

"He let them go a long time ago, and we let him go. He said he had to search for his feelings or some such. Started preaching false doctrine. He had some odd ideas about dying and about how he wanted to die. I don't really talk about that 'cause I don't understand it much."

"Where does he live?" Brett said.

"Marvel Creek," Judith said, "but you don't need to talk to him. He doesn't know a thing about the children after Thomas was twelve and Jackrabbit was thirteen. Didn't deal with them at all. Besides, we don't really know where he lives over there."

"Christianity sure holds the family together, don't it?" Leonard said.

I saw Thomas move as if he might get out of the chair, which was exactly what Leonard wanted. He gave Leonard a hard look that melted fast as a snowflake on a hot stove, and he suddenly found more comfort in the chair than before, located a spot on the window behind Brett and concentrated on that. My guess was being here with us was his idea of hell turned true.

After a few more questions from Brett, they gave her a fistful of money that was mostly ones and fives and would cover about two days' work. They promised more just as soon as Thomas got paid over at the chicken plant, a place where I had worked briefly. I didn't tell him we had the same alma mater.

They got up and left. Brett picked up Judith's tablet and stared at it.

"There goes the fucking Madonna on earth and one of her little fucking shit-ass scamps," Leonard said.

"Truth is, I feel sorry for them," Brett said.

"Me too," I said. "For a minute."

5

For lunch, we went to an El Salvadorean place that had only been open a short time and had been built inside of what was once a tire-and-lube business. They had rickety tables and rickety chairs and really good food there. The tires had long been vacated, in case you were curious, and I presumed there was no lube business going on in any manner, shape, or form.

I had my favorite meal, jalapeños and cheese wrapped in grilled bacon with a side of rice and charro beans and a chicken tamale wrapped in a plantain husk, along with plantain chips for the table. Brett had chicken quesadillas, and Leonard had an enchilada about the size of a pontoon boat. I don't know what the people at the table near us had, but they seemed to be enjoying it.

"The father," Brett said. "They didn't say much about him, but I think we ought to start there, find out who he is. He's in the same town where Jackie disappeared. That's quite a coincidence. He could be hiding her. She could have gone there looking for him, and in fact, that makes a lot of sense."

"Their dislike of him kind of shuts off their thinking," I said.

"I don't believe they had a lot of thinking to shut off," Leonard said. "I'm surprised they got the brain cells to remind their bodies to breathe."

"Our dislike of them might shut off our thinking, now that I consider it," I said.

"Sucks to be them," Leonard said. "But, yeah, dear old Dad might have seen Jackrabbit last. For all we know she's living in Marvel Creek selling antiques, is married to a Klan Grand Wizard, and has four kids and a pet goat, all with bodies covered in tattoos and their own nine-millimeter pistols, including the goat."

"Goats prefer something lighter," I said. "Maybe a twenty-five-caliber. Goes with their outfit."

"Boys, that's enough," Brett said. "What I'm thinking is you and Leonard go to Marvel Creek. I'll see if I can find some of the others on this list. Chance comes in this afternoon, and I'll get her to help me. The Internet ought to be for something other than me looking up photos of men with huge dicks."

"Zing," Leonard said.

I ignored both of them.

"Well, we got his name, so we can get started," Leonard said. "Sebastian Mulhaney. What a name."

"Beats Jackrabbit," I said. "Drop us off at my car, hon, and we'll go. You can make phone calls and find addresses. Me and Leonard are people persons."

"You, maybe. Leonard, not so much," Brett said. "And I'm not that sure about you."

"This is true," Leonard said. "Nobody likes me and I don't like nobody. I hope they all get ants in their ass."

6

I rolled us into Marvel Creek about three o'clock in the afternoon on a warm day with a dry wind blowing. Way to the west,
clouds were brewing like darkened beer suds, bundling up rain-
drops, rolling them slowly in our direction.

I grew up in Marvel Creek. Before I was born it had been a
rough but thriving oil town, back in the thirties, then it became a
rough played-out oil town in the fifties. It was made up of the de-
scendants of oil-field trash, as they sometimes called themselves,
thugs, prostitutes, pimps and gamblers, a few lucky oil tycoons.
Back then, unless you were one of the lucky ones who struck it
rich and stayed rich, it was a town where broken dreams got even
more broken and crawled off to die in the river bottoms.

You were on the poor end of things, the blue-collar end of
things, you saw stuff the better-off folks didn't see and sometimes
refused to admit existed. Things the cops didn't always report and
were actually sometimes responsible for. Black bodies, wrapped
in chains, slipped off into the muddy Sabine; women and wives

who wore black eyes so often they might have been part raccoon. Fights and bad deeds, enough to fill a thousand books, things done in the dark, and on the river, and in the deep green woods, even deeper back then, before lumber mills became pulp-wood serial killers and ravaged trees in the name of progress and the almighty dollar.

That muddy brown river winds along at one end of town, crawling under a long bridge, pushing mud and snakes and fish and debris all the way to the Gulf of Mexico. I spent a lot of time along that river and on it in rowboats and motorboats and even inner tubes. Once, long ago when we were young, me and Leonard even found a sunken boat out there with bodies in it.

Another time my ex-wife got us into some bad business searching for treasure in the river. We found the treasure, but in the end, it brought more pain than satisfaction.

Back then, when you crossed the bridge on your way out, you came to Hell's Half Mile, a line of honky-tonks full of drunken patrons trying to wash down poverty, bad marriages, and gone-to-hell children. Whores worked there, taking customers to little trailers out back. There was no family night.

Knives and guns came out on many occasions, mostly on Saturday nights. The altercation might have to do with some whore's attentions or with patrons' differing political views or their disagreements on the finer points of religion ("Love thy neighbor" with a load of lead or a sharp knife), but mostly it had to do with bottled-up rage from being poor and knowing full well there had to be something better than a life of hard work, hot nights, and empty bottles, and knowing too that if there was, you weren't going to get a taste of it. Mix it all with alcohol, and it was like trying to blend fire with gasoline.

In time, to the delight of churchgoing women and to the disappointment of beer drinkers and whoremongers, the tonks went out of business. The whores and the pimps and the shooters and knife fighters went with them or ended up on the school board, and the former patrons drank at home. The old buildings were burned down for the insurance money or turned weather-beaten and vacant.

Not so many people ran the river and the woods like before. A great used-book store had grown up in the town. It nearly took up an entire block, giving way on one corner to a Mexican restaurant. The restaurant's site had been a bank when I was a kid. The town was now known for antiques. It had become respectable.

Respectable place or not, driving around it always made me tremble a bit, like the past was blowing a cold wind over my heart. Always got the impression that the old world I had known was still out there, just one bloody scratch below the surface, and all it took was the right incantation to release it.

Or merely the arrival of good ole us, Hap and Leonard.

7

Brett sent to my phone the address she found for Jackrabbit's daddy. We put the address into the GPS and drove over there.

To our surprise, it was a church. When I was young it had been a theater. I had watched many a movie there, had seen cowboys and Indians ride, vampires suck blood, monsters jump out of the shadows, and I had seen crime shows, musicals, and stories of romance. Those days were gone.

There were white crosses painted on the old glass doors, the ticket booth had a wooden barrier over the ticket slot, and the door that led into the booth from inside the theater was now a solid piece of wall. Where garish movie posters had once filled frames on either side of the outside theater archway were now posters of a different sort of garishness, one with Jesus on the cross. The crown of thorns on his forehead had thorns the size of tenpenny nails stuck into his flesh, causing blood to leak down his face and drip over his lips. Beneath Jesus, a Roman soldier who looked a lot like John Wayne was holding a spear and was looking up at him on the cross with an expression of either satisfaction, boredom, or wonder. Maybe they were discussing the weather.

"Hey, you're going to get wet up there," says the soldier.

"Hell, don't I know it," says Jesus back.

On the other side of the building, there was a less dramatic poster with Jesus standing on a high place looking up to the heavens. People sat on the ground near him, looking where he was looking, and there were sheep and lambs looking up as well, unaware that they might soon be decorating a plate with some fig jelly.

We pulled on the front door, but it was locked, so we went around back, down an alley composed of cracked bricks, and found a door there that was wide open.

"It's not breaking and entering if the door is open," Leonard said.

"Way I heard it," I said.

For a moment we stood there, considering, then finally went inside. It was deep dark in there and I used the flashlight on my phone to guide us down a space where odds and ends had been kept, and were still kept, but now those odds and ends were not movie-related. There were hymnbooks and Bibles, some of them quite ragged, and a number of cardboard boxes containing who knew what.

After a few moments, the hallway terminated at a door, one of those you push against. We pushed and came into the theater itself. It was lit up as bright as a visit to the sun, and it was cold with air-conditioning, the way a theater ought to be. I turned off my phone light.

The old theater seats were still there, but they had been reupholstered, and the carpet between the seats no longer sucked at your shoes due to sticky soda spills. It was bright red again and soft.

There was a guy on his knee, leaning into an aisle seat, his head out of sight. An elbow appeared from time to time, moving back and forth. We heard a soft clicking sound.

"Hello, the theater," Leonard said.

The man stopped doing what he was doing and came to his feet. He had a staple gun in his hand.

"Sorry to barge in," I said. "The door was open."

"Quite all right," the man said. "I opened it to bring some stuff in, forgot to close it."

The man was about six five, broad-shouldered, with a bit of belly that anyone with any sense and experience would know wouldn't slow him down if he decided to pull your head off and shit down your neck. He had a well-trimmed black beard and longish black hair that fell down his neck and over his ears. I guess he was about my age, give or take a year or two.

We walked up to him.

"Can I help you gentlemen?" he said.

"Hope so," I said, and stuck out my hand. He placed the stapler on the closest theater seat, shook my hand, then shook Leonard's.

"I was stapling upholstery on some of the seats."

"I used to come here to watch movies," I said.

"Ah, me too," he said. "Wait a minute. Aren't you Hap Collins?"

"I am."

"You remember me?"

"Sorry."

"Gary Jamesway."

"You played football. I think you were a year behind me."

"It was baseball, and I wasn't very good at it."

"Not the way I remember it," I said. I had never really kept up with baseball, but there was talk about Jamesway all the time. I remembered it now. Yeah. Baseball, not football. "You went pro, right?"

"I was okay when we played who we played in high school. Graduated, got a chance with the Astros, but it turned out that against someone who could really throw, I couldn't hit, and against someone who could really hit, I couldn't catch, and I couldn't run fast enough to match anybody. I was a high-school whiz and a professional dud. I warmed a bench for a couple of seasons, then they let me go, and I was glad of it. Haven't picked up a baseball since."

"At least you got to the show," Leonard said.

"Yeah," Jamesway said, "there was that."

"You're not actually who we're looking for," I said, "but glad to see you."

"Who are you looking for?"

I told him.

"Oh my, Sebastian. May the Lord watch over his confused and tortured soul."

"I'm thinking Sebastian's story isn't a happy one," Leonard said.

"Might say it has a weird ending."

"I thought he lived here," I said. "Or preached here."

"He did, once. I own the place now. I'm the preacher. Actually, I was the preacher a year before he left. He stopped showing up to preach, and when I started, I lost most of his flock, but in a short time I got a new one. It's growing all the time. New people are coming in. The things he taught, they couldn't stand the bright of the light."

"That so," Leonard said.

"Some years back I came here and heard him preach, and I didn't like him. Stayed after one of his sermons and talked to him about, how shall I say, being more Christ-like and less Joshua-like, since being Christians, we weren't supposed to be worshipping the old ways, but the new ways of Jesus. You see, he talked the Old Testament and tossed in lizard men from time to time."

"Say what?" Leonard said.

"He and a large portion of his flock were what you might call conspiracy theorists. They didn't require proof, only a need they wanted to fulfill. Something in their lives that was more interesting than braces on their kids' teeth, nursing a hangover, or paying bills while navigating a changing world. They weren't up to it. But if they could believe lizard men were out there, messing everything up for the rest of us, they could have a satisfying creepy feeling that was preferable to an unsatisfying feeling of boredom and routine and unimportance."

"His wife said he was a Presbyterian," I said.

"Hardly," Jamesway said, and laughed.

"So you told him he was full of it," I said, "and that lizard men had yet to show up, and he said, 'How about you preach?'"

"He was starting to fall apart. Had a lot of hate and disappointment in him. Didn't really seem to care about much at that point. He surprised me by offering me a chance to give a sermon the next Sunday. I didn't know it then, but he was looking for a way to get out of his responsibilities, and I came at the right time. His crowd was not my crowd. They left, and I stayed, and Sebastian stayed. But in the back. Drinking most of the time. Then a young woman came around for a while, and then she stopped coming, and he went away. Short time after that they found his remains in Davy Crockett National Forest. A hiker came across it. His corpse was in bad shape, but they could tell his chest had been split open, his ribs separated with a hammer. His heart and some other organs were missing, and they didn't think it was decay or animals that got to them."

"Damn lizard men," Leonard said.

Jamesway smiled.

"The grave he was in was deep and wide, but it had eroded. He had that wound in his chest and a jump rope around his neck. They concluded he was strangled with that, which considering they found it wrapped around his neck a couple of times doesn't sound like great police deduction to me. A cocker spaniel could have figured that out. He had his hands in the pockets of his pants, like he was relaxing. The bones of his hands, actually. Like he'd stuck them in there and held them there while he was strangled."

I was surprised Brett hadn't found Sebastian's death notice on the Internet, and I said so to Jamesway.

"It was just this week he was confirmed dead, but they figured he'd been dead for a couple weeks, give or take a weekend. No one went to the trouble to put an obituary in the paper. I didn't bother with it either, I'm ashamed to say. I don't know why I even came to this church. I like to think God had plans for me."

"What I want to know, is there any money in it?" Leonard said.

Jamesway laughed a little. It wasn't something that would turn contagious, but there was humor there.

"Not that much. Not unless you want to be a giant blowhard like some evangelists are, always assuring you of a place in heaven if you'll send them money. People can be easily conned out of their possessions and their common sense if you use religion as a lever. I don't believe like that. Sebastian made a deal with me to

37

buy the place. I got a loan, and I'm paying it off. Got it for a song. He had my money when we left the real estate agent's office, or the check, anyway. When they found him, he didn't have a check, or any money at all. Hey, let's go up front to the office. I got coffee there, and I'm ready for some."

8

We tagged along through the side door that led out of the main part of the theater and into a lobby that seemed so much smaller to me than in my memory. Fact was, the whole theater seemed a miniature of how I recalled it. I missed the smell of hot buttered popcorn and the way drinks fizzed in paper cups and made your nose hairs twitch. I missed being ten years old.

In Jamesway's office, which was a bit tight, we sat on some fold-out chairs, and he settled in behind a cheap desk after he started the coffeemaker. The desk shook a little when he put his arms on it.

"This place, Hap, remember the black folks had to go up into the balcony, weren't allowed on the bottom floor?" Jamesway said.

"Of course I remember," I said.

"Black people wanted to go to the restroom," Jamesway said, "they had to leave the theater, walk across the street to a concrete bunker with a sign painted over it that said COLORED.

"In high school, I heard from a guy, older than both of us, Hap, that had been a part-time usher here, back when they had ushers, and he said the carpet in the balcony stank of urine. He was angry about it, people peeing on the carpet. He said, 'That's how those people are. Animals.' But he didn't have to cross the street to pee. Didn't have to miss a big chunk of the movie."

"Suppose all this nostalgia you're giving out is because Sebastian wasn't as forward-thinking as you," Leonard said. "We got the idea he left his family because his views had become more mainstream, but you say that ain't so."

"If he was more mainstream than they liked, then they must be way on the far edge of the cliff."

"Right there at the very edge," Leonard said, "looking into the abyss. And I'm wishing they'd fall in, except we gave our word we'd work for them."

"That means something to you, giving your word?" Jamesway asked.

"It means a lot," Leonard said. "I keep my word until the people who I gave my word to break theirs."

"Fair enough," Jamesway said. "Let me tell you, Sebastian was crazy, talking about lizard men and the apocalypse on the horizon. Worse, he had folks listening to him. For a time, this was a kind of place where people who hated anything different in the social order since 1950 could come and say things they might be reluctant to say out in the open. They hated immigrants, black people, and anyone they considered liberal or progressive. They thought women were deemed by God to be of service to them."

Jamesway got up and grabbed some cups out of a cabinet, poured us some of the coffee, asked how we liked it. We told him. He used artificial creamer and artificial sweetener to fix it up. The coffee tasted like someone had steeped a dead gerbil in it. I drank more than I wanted so as to be polite. I hoped the gerbil had clean feet.

"And what exactly is your denomination?" I said.

"Church of Jesus," he said. "It's new."

"You mean you made it up?" Leonard said.

"Pretty much," he said. "All religions are made up, or they're modifications of what's gone before. I try and teach what some might call a progressive view of the Bible, what others might call blasphemy. There are more people moving in a positive direction than a negative, and I founded my church on that."

"You must not pay attention to elections," I said.

"I believe in people."

"That must take a real job of work, plus overtime," Leonard said.

"It's kind of what my job is," Jamesway said. "Believing and hope. I don't think Noah sailed around with an ark full of animals or that Moses parted the Red Sea, and I'm not even sure Jesus was divine, but I like his message. That's what I believe in."

"And that works for your congregation?" I said.

"I leave out that part about not being sure of Jesus being divine because I think the rest of it is worth it. I don't teach from the Old Testament at all, only the New. But you want to know about Sebastian?"

"Only so we can look for someone else," Leonard said. "His daughter."

"Ah, Jackie," he said. "Called her Jackrabbit."

"That's the one," Leonard said.

"She's the girl I mentioned who came around—well, woman. Interesting character, Jackie. Grew up with Sebastian and her mother and her brother, who, and I shouldn't say such a thing as a servant of God, but if he was a lightbulb he wouldn't light up the inside of a frog's ass. I'm basing this mostly on what Jackie told me, of course, but he and his mother came here asking about Jackie, Sebastian too. I told them a lot less than I'm telling you. I got bad vibes from the brother. Felt what Jackie'd told me, he confirmed. He was really irked she had been with black men. He felt the family honor had been diminished."

"Their honor was diminished when they were born," Leonard said.

"Well, mother and son have their heads firmly up their asses, but in their own way, they have a code they live by," Jamesway said.

"Hitler lived by a code," Leonard said. "But that didn't keep it from being a bad one."

"Point taken," Jamesway said.

"You didn't say you knew Jackie all that well before, but now you're saying you did," I said. "Before she was just a girl that came around."

"I didn't say I didn't know her," Jamesway said. "I was trying to say I didn't know her when she was first coming around to see Sebastian. She came back later, after he left. Ended up confiding in me soon as she figured out I wasn't someone who was supporting the nonsense Sebastian had been preaching. Jackie was different from her people. She was smart as a whip with numbers, helped me with some tax returns and the like a few times.

"As far as her father was concerned, she could have been a stray dog with the mange. He ignored her, wouldn't pay attention to her. Me and her went out a few times. Nothing serious. Grabbed a burger, went to a movie. I learned she had been with a man named Ace, and she said there was another fellow had a serious crush on her, and she kind of liked him. He had money. I hate to make Jackie sound like a gold digger, but I think she was looking for security. She didn't grow up with much of that. That's why it was best she gave up on Sebastian as a father, if for no other reason than he became obsessed with death."

"How so?" I said.

"You can fix this idea up with roast nuts and fill the air with incense, and it will still seem messed up and stinky. He wanted someone to murder him. Wanted it done in a specific way. And considering how his body was found, how it was worked over, he certainly convinced someone to help him out. That's what I meant earlier when I said I had some idea."

"A form of assisted suicide," I said.

"I really don't know how to split that hair," he said. "Helping someone buy the rope isn't quite the same thing as putting it around that person's neck and then cutting him open and busting his ribs out of the way to take his heart and a key."

"That's what he asked you to do?" I said.

"That's what he asked. Said he'd pay me to do it. Told me what he wanted to do and said he was going to have a grave ready in Davy Crockett National Forest, wanted to put his hands in his pockets while I strangled him to make him weak, and then he wanted me to cut him open while he was still alive, use a hammer to break his ribs so I could get to his stomach. He was going to swallow a key right before he was to be strangled. He kept talking about how he wanted to see his guts steam in the air. He was obsessed with that. Seeing his intestines. Wanted them laid out on his chest so he could see them as he died. Said the key in his stomach would go to a bank box, and the box would contain half the money he promised; other half would be given to me before killing him in the manner he asked. Craziest thing I ever heard of. I didn't take the bait and tried to counsel him, but he wasn't having any of that. His mind was made up. Still, I never thought he'd find someone who'd go through with it. I thought he would drop it in time."

"Tell the police this?" I said.

"Right after Sebastian was found."

"And?"

"Chief didn't think anyone would pay someone to murder them. But they were curious about how I would know about the body, how it was found. Had their eye on me for a while, since I knew things that hadn't been released to the news. I think they've given up on me now. I don't even own a car, so how would I get out there to kill and bury him?"

"I don't understand why he didn't just kill himself," Leonard said.

"Isn't merely about suicide," Jamesway said. "There's a name for it, but I don't know what it is. People like him are looking for someone to make them suffer. They get off on it sexually. Suppose it has something to do with self-loathing. I don't know. No expert on that kind of thing."

"How much did he offer you?" Leonard said.

"Ten thousand dollars. Said he'd give me five up-front, the rest would be in the bank box at the bank here. There's only one. He was offering me some of the money I had used to pay for this place. Maybe he thought that would be an incentive. Getting part of my money back.

"I told him, 'What if you give your killer the first half and they don't do it? Or what if they just shoot you in the head and ignore the ritual?' That didn't deter him. He was willing to chance it. I think the fantasy was so intense he couldn't shake it. That was his idea of the ultimate orgasm."

"Damn," Leonard said.

"Was a key found inside of Sebastian?" I asked.

Jamesway shrugged. "Don't know."

"Did they check the bank box?" I asked.

"I don't know that either, but my guess is yes. Maybe the police chief has five thousand dollars in his bank account now, or maybe whoever did it got the key like they were supposed to."

"That's some messed-up shit," Leonard said. "Jackrabbit, do you know where she is?"

Jamesway shook his head. "Not anymore. Last time I saw her, she was in deep despair. Tried to talk to me about it. I tried to listen. But she could never get it out. It was as if she were trying to cough up an anvil. She sat right where you're sitting, Hap. She opened her mouth but nothing would come out. I suggested therapy, told her I might know someone. Haven't heard from her since. She was an odd duck, but I like odd ducks, unless they're as odd as her father. He was less like a duck and more like a vulture."

"What was Jackie's job?" I asked.

"She kept books for a local company," he said. "New Paradise. I think she did accounting, but she wasn't an accountant. Just good with numbers. She told me once her mother thought she might be a witch, way she could figure things with numbers. Math, like gravity, is hard for those kinds of folks to grasp as reality."

"Do you happen to have a recent photo of Jackie?" I said.

"No...wait. There's a photo we took of the congregation at

Christmas. She was here, trying to get in with her dad, trying to find some connection, you know. You think something happened to her?"

"We don't have any opinions right now," I said.

He opened his desk drawer and took out a stack of photos. He thumbed through them. "Here it is."

He handed the photo to Leonard, who looked at it, then leaned over and showed it to me.

There were a dozen people in it. I spotted Jackie right off. She was on the left side of the photo. It wasn't a great picture, and she might have been a little too thin, but she looked quite pretty. She was dressed up, high heels. Her hair was longer, falling below her shoulders. She was smiling. I could see those jackrabbit teeth for sure, but they fit her somehow.

"Pretty, isn't she," Jamesway said. "Unusual-looking. Believe me, I was hoping for more for us than there was. She was so worried about her father, about connecting to him, we couldn't find solid ground to stand on together. She wanted friendship, and I wanted something else. That said, there was always something about Jackie that made me think if you stood on ground too close to her, it would shift."

All the faces in the photo were white except one. A big black man with a shaved head and a smile so forced, all that was missing was a gun to his head.

I put the photo on Jamesway's desk and tapped a finger on it. "Who's this?" I had an idea what the answer might be.

"Ah, that's Ace. An old boyfriend of hers. Wouldn't have been in Sebastian's congregation, I can promise you that. Ace and Jackie had a thing once, when this was picture was taken. She outgrew him. She was outgrowing everyone she knew from the old days. Was about to start at Tyler Junior College, go on to the University of Texas branch there. Least that's what she said. Thing holding her back a little was a connection she wanted with her father. My guess is that's what she wanted to talk about the day she was here and couldn't do it. That and the baby."

"Baby?" I said.

"Yeah. She didn't want to stay with the father. Guess it was Ace's kid. I held Jackie while she cried about it all, and then she went away, and later she wasn't pregnant, but there wasn't any kid. I don't know what happened there. False alarm, maybe. Miscarriage."

"Could she already be in Tyler, for college?" I said.

"Said she was registering this fall, but that doesn't mean she isn't there already. Could be anywhere, I guess."

"Do you know about someone named George?"

"Nope, can't say I do."

"She lived with him for a while," I said.

"Never mentioned him to me," he said.

"Could we get an address where she lived?"

"I suppose that would be all right," Jamesway said. "I can tell you where she lived. I don't even know if the landlord knows she's gone yet. It's near here. I walked by her place, just in case she might still be around, knocked on the door, but she didn't answer. Truck wasn't there. I peeked through a window. Looked abandoned."

"Could she have just been out?" I said.

"I doubt it. I went by a couple times after that. No one was there. I think her rent is still paid up."

He wrote her old address down for us, the make and color of her truck as well.

"Thanks for your time," I said, and me and Leonard stood up.

"We have services during the week," Jamesway said, "if you want to sample my style of preaching."

"Nope," Leonard said. "I got enough misery in my life without adding religion to it."

9

As we left the church and drove to Jackrabbit's address, Leonard said, "What do you think?"

"About Jamesway?"

"No, about the price of wedding dresses. Yes. Jamesway."

"He seems all right, and that story about Sebastian is so wild, I believe it. Who'd make up shit like that? But I don't know if everything he said was true. Guy walks into a racist church, and next thing you know he's running it, minus the racism and lizard men? I don't know. As for Jackie, yeah, I think he had a crush on her, but where is she? How much did he really know about her?"

"Here's what I got to consider, Hap. What if Jamesway did take Sebastian up on his offer? That money would be a real boon to a fellow who is obviously living on a shoestring. Doesn't even own a car. That coffee we had, it had been run through the filter more than once."

"Maybe he likes it that way," I said. "And if he had the money, don't you think he'd buy him a fresh batch of coffee?"

"What about Jackrabbit? Where is she? Maybe she and her dad weren't so far apart on things. Maybe she's the one did him in for the money, and to please her crazy papa. Might be why she was upset when Jamesway spoke to her last, upset over what she'd done."

"Could be," I said.

"Shit, man. I don't recognize the world anymore."

The place where Jackie had been living was a little blue house on a clean street with simple houses of varying sizes and colors. The blue house was a nice enough house. The cobblestoned walk was lined with untrimmed shrubs, and a fat black cat was squatting in between a couple of them, taking a dump. The cat didn't bother to scamper as we came up. It gave us the cold eye as we moved along the walk past it, like we were the royal wipers falling down on the job.

We stopped under the porch overhang and I knocked. No one answered.

Leonard walked over and looked in the empty carport, knocked on the door that led from it to the house. No one answered that knock either.

We walked to the back of the house and found another door, knocked there. Nothing.

Looking around, we saw there was a backyard fence. It was the neighbor's fence, not one that belonged to Jackie's rental, but it blocked easy sight of us at the rear of the house. To the left were shrubs and another house. On the other side was a grassy section, and beyond you could see a street, and beyond that the old red-brick Piggly Wiggly that had closed down when I was in high school. No other business had replaced it. An old car motored by on that street, coughed around a corner, and moved out of sight.

"How fast can you pick a lock?" I said.

"Fast enough," Leonard said. He pulled his lock-picking kit out of his pocket but hesitated. He tried the door. It was unlocked.

"Fast enough for you?" Leonard said.

"Plenty fast," I said, and we slipped inside and shut the door.

The air was thick and warm and a little sticky, had that musty odor a house gets that's been closed up for a while with no one living there. There was furniture in the room, most of it of the bargain-basement variety.

We went past a kitchen table and some cheap kitchen chairs with plastic seats and backs with butterfly designs on the plastic. Very festive. We entered the bedroom, and because I am an ace detective, I noticed it was empty. No bed. No end tables. Nothing. The closet door was thrown open, and all that was in there was some dust.

Leonard said, "You hear that?"

"What?"

He put a finger to his mouth and became very still. When he spoke, it was softly. "Someone just came in the back door."

Before we could move out of the bedroom, the doorway filled with a shape about the size of a grizzly bear in platform shoes. The bear had on a red-and-white knit cap with ears on it, bear ears, of course, and he was carrying one of the kitchen chairs. Bear or no bear, he had entered the house and the room with no more noise than a polite lady folding a Kleenex. Before I could say a word or do a thing, he hit me with the chair.

10

He hit me a good lick. Even cheap chairs are surprisingly sturdy. It knocked me down. I tried to get up, but the floor wouldn't let me. It was holding me back. My shoulder, which had taken the brunt of the blow, felt as if it were missing, and my reflexes had taken a vacation. My forehead had intercepted a bit of the chair as well. It ached.

As Leonard charged him, the chair swung through the air again, but Leonard ducked low. The chair passed over him, and he rushed the bear, caught his legs near the ankles, and hit him in the groin with his head, which knocked him back on his ass, causing him to lose his bear-ear hat and his grip on the chair. The chair slid across the floor, hit the far wall with its legs, and bounced back toward us. That chair was aggressive.

The bear had enough savvy and experience, or had watched enough mixed martial arts, to wrap his legs around Leonard and squeeze him between them.

Before the bear could go for a move of some sort, Leonard

snapped both of his elbows back and into the bear's inner thighs, causing him to grunt and drop his legs. Leonard got a knee up and in the bear's balls, grabbed the bear's left leg, and passed it quickly over his head, rolling the beast onto his belly. Then Leonard was on the bear's back, slamming a right and then a left hook into his head.

"That's for Hap," Leonard said.

I felt that was very thoughtful.

"Damn, that hurt," the bear said.

"You ought to try being hit by a chair," I said.

By that time the floor was nice enough to relinquish some gravity so I could sit with my legs crossed. The room was still moving a bit.

The bear had his hands over the back of his head, trying to protect himself.

"You done, shit-ass?" Leonard said.

"I'm done," the bear said. "Done." He sounded like a kid who had just been whipped by his mother for playing in the mud while wearing his Sunday go-to-meeting clothes.

I was considerably better by that point. My head hurt, but I was in control of my legs. The room wasn't spinning anymore. I got up, went over, and squatted down near the bear. He couldn't raise his head comfortably with Leonard on his back, but with me in my squatting position, he could hear me quite well.

"I got a question, Ace."

"How do you know my name?"

"I'll do the questions, you do the answers. Why the fuck did you hit me with a goddamn chair?"

"This ain't your house," Ace said.

"Isn't yours either," I said.

"You don't know that," Ace said.

"I'm a pretty good guesser. Were you looking for Jackie?"

"You know her?"

"We do," I said. "Kind of. And we know who you are."

"Yeah, calling me by my name sort of gave me the idea you might. But how do you know me?"

"You look as ugly as you did in the shitty photograph we saw," Leonard said.

Ace said to me, "Can you get this gorilla off my back?"

"Is that racist?" I asked Leonard. "Calling you a gorilla?"

"No one would ever think a man as handsome as me might resemble a gorilla," Leonard said. "But you know, sometimes that is an insult for black folk."

"Why I'm asking," I said.

"What the fuck?" Ace said. "I'm black too."

"Damn, Leonard. He is black."

"Then we got to say it wasn't meant racist," Leonard said.

"Shall you get off his back?" I said.

"Ace," Leonard said. "I'm going to get up, and if you try to move and get frisky, I'm going to beat your ass flat as my line of credit."

Leonard stood up, then bent and frisked Ace for weapons, didn't find any. Ace remained on the floor.

Leonard stepped away from Ace, looked at me, said, "Hap, you all right?"

"Close enough to it," I said.

"You want me to hit him with the chair?" Leonard said. "Would that make you feel better?"

"Naw, it's cool," I said.

Ace remained on his stomach. Leonard righted the chair, pulled it up close to Ace, and sat down on it.

"Now," I said, "why-for-how-come did you hit me with a god-damn chair? And let's keep our answers to the point, because I'm in a bad mood, and you put me there."

"I thought y'all was thieves, coming up in here."

"What are we going to steal?" I said. "Those nice kitchen chairs, the shitty table? Couple dust motes out of the closet?"

"I don't know," Ace said. "I was hoping it was Jackrabbit, then I seen you two."

"You could have said howdy," I said. "Where I come from, it's a nicer greeting than hitting someone with a fucking chair."

"All right, then, I'm sorry."

"My head hurts anyway."

Leonard hummed a few bars of Kasey Lansdale's song "Sorry Ain't Enough."

"I hear that," I said. "And agree."

"What?" Ace said.

Leonard tapped Ace on the ribs with the toe of his boot. "I can tell you're no music lover."

"Hadn't knocked me down," Ace said, "I'd have whipped both your asses."

"Yeah," I said. "So you're saying if Leonard hadn't whipped your ass you'd have whipped his, and mine too? Well, hell, dumbass. If the world wasn't turning we could all get off. You can sit up now."

"But do it easy and don't get cute," Leonard said. "You might not be as big and able as you like to imagine."

11

We ended up in the kitchen. I took the chair that had been used to whack me and placed it at the table and sat on it as a kind of vengeance. Leonard stood with his arms crossed and leaned against the wall near where Ace sat.

Ace had retrieved that ridiculous hat and it was resting on his knee. I knew from the way Leonard eyed it, he wanted one. It had a tie on either side that could be used to bind it under the chin.

"You hit me hard," he said to Leonard.

"Yep," Leonard said. "And I can do it again."

"I'm starting to think I should have let Leonard hit you with this chair," I said.

"Look here, Ace," Leonard said. "Let's bury the hatchet. Door was open when we came. We're here looking for Jackie— Jackrabbit—on account we were hired by her mother and brother to find her."

"Well, that's something," Ace said, looking at Leonard. "Was you wearing whiteface when her family showed up?"

"They wanted me to," Leonard said.

"What the fuck, then, man?" Ace said. "Why would you work for them fucking peckerwoods?"

"Money spends either way, no account for color," Leonard said.

"And they wanted to know about their daughter," I said. "I thought if she was missing and something was wrong, we ought to find out. Seemed like the right thing to do."

"One of you works for money, and the other one is some kind of knight?"

"We both spend the money," Leonard said. "You came here looking for her, so you expected her to be here."

Ace shook his head gently. I figured it hurt too much for him to shake it hard.

"I came by here even though I knew she was gone, but then I seen your car at the curb. I tried the doors, and the back one was unlocked. I came in and found y'all, and I thought maybe you had something to do with her missing."

"And your immediate solution was to hit me with a chair," I said.

"I didn't know if you had guns or not," Ace said. "I didn't know if you was all right or not."

"You'll have to take our word," I said. "We're all right. All we want to do is find Jackie."

"Still don't like the idea of that brother of hers seeing her again," Ace said, "and neither does she. You ought to keep that in mind while you're looking for her. He's dangerous. Got some old ideas."

"We find her, we won't make her go home," I said. "We'll just make sure she's okay and tell our clients she's fine or she isn't, and then Jackie can do what she wants. I think it's fair enough that even a couple of racist assholes ought to know what happened to their loved one. And if you know something about where she is or what happened to her, and you don't tell us, we might have to think you got something to do with her not being around. That could look bad for you. We got some friends in LaBorde who are cops, and they got friends all over the place. We tell some kind of story that includes you in a starring role, some people might believe it."

"He means you might go to jail, you did something or not," Leonard said. "No charge for the translation."

"I ain't done nothing with her, man. I been looking for her. I come by here just like I said. Seen your car, thought she might be with someone else. Don't know exactly what I thought. I came in and heard y'all, picked up a chair, and hit Whitey with it."

"And Whitey didn't like it," I said.

"When did you see her last?" Leonard said.

"I don't mark it on the calendar. Me and her, we had a thing going, you know, and her mother and that fucked-up brother didn't like it. He threatened me once and pulled a knife. I hit him with a chair."

"Seriously," I said.

"Yep."

"You like chairs," I said.

"Thomas never mentioned you two had a confrontation," Leonard said. "That didn't come up."

"Still happened," Ace said. "Bet he didn't mention getting his ass handed to him."

"But really," I said, "a chair? You go around hitting everyone with a chair?"

"It was handy. Me and her, we done all right, even had a kid.

58

I think that fucking preacher might have talked her out of staying with me."

"That's not his story," Leonard said.

"He's probably got a lot of stories," Ace said.

"We heard about the kid and the miscarriage," I said. "Sorry."

"Shit, there wasn't any miscarriage," Ace said. "Kid got born. I didn't see it much, and I don't even know what she named it. She went back to Junkyard George for a while. Found out he was the same asshole he was when she left him the first time. She wouldn't tell me nothing about the baby. Said that wasn't my concern no more."

None of this fit anything we had been told so far.

"Take it you weren't hanging with the white folks when her dad was preaching at the old picture show," Leonard said.

"I couldn't get in that church then. Jackrabbit's father would have shot my ass and told how a wild nigger come up in there to rob him, and he'd most likely been believed. Folks in this town ain't entirely civilized, you know what I mean?"

"You knew Sebastian, though?" I said.

"Knew who he was," Ace said. "I came to the church after he sold it to that other fellow, Jamesway. Listened to a couple of Jamesway's sermons, but I wasn't thinking Jesus. I was trying to get back with Jackrabbit. And they had free cookies on Wednesday, and some really bad coffee. I tell you this, and I'm serious, don't drink the fucking coffee over there."

"Too late," Leonard said.

"Ain't it bad?" Ace said.

"The worst," Leonard said.

"Sebastian ever threaten you, say anything to you about being with Jackie?" I said.

"Like I said, didn't go up in there when he was running the show. Went later, when Jamesway came in. Her father still lived in the back then but didn't have no say about who came and went anymore. Spent his time drinking, until one day he's gone. Then there's stories about what happened to him, and then Jackie's gone."

"Stories?" Leonard said, knowing full well what Ace meant. But we wanted to hear him say it.

"Stories about how he was killed. Talk about how he had himself killed in a fucked-up kind of way. Never heard of nobody doing something like that. Don't know I believe it. Course, he'd offered money to have it done, so a person might make an exception. Fucker wasn't exactly lovable. Before it went down, when me and Jackrabbit was together, she told me how her father's favorite part of the Bible was where Jesus got whipped, nailed on the cross, and stuck with a spear. He told her with Jesus on the cross like that, had to have pissed and shit himself, 'cause that's what would happen. He liked all that pain and death, piss and shit. He wanted to have something like it, to die slow and in pain."

"How'd Jackie take what happened to her dad?" I said.

"Pretty well, actually. By then, think she was glad he was gone. She tried to get this daughter-and-daddy thing going, but she might as well have been invisible. Her being pregnant didn't move him off the dime either, it being a black baby. Never did find out what happened to my kid, but I will. Hell, I think I'd do better than Jackie raising a kid."

"You don't look like the dedicated-father type to me," I said.

"Shit. You don't know me none at all. Jackrabbit had some fucked-up ideas. All she thought about was numbers and diagrams and shit. She was always saying how numbers and diagrams could explain anything except emotions. That's the way she put it. Something would come up now and again, and she'd say something about this or that, and I'd think, Damn, that gal has stripped a gear. She'd say how she could move between dimensions or some such shit and how in one of them she was happy as a pig in shit, and in this one, not so much. She'd go to the good one when she needed to be happy, but she came back to this one to be mad. Claimed you could do that 'cause it could be explained by numbers, but I don't see it. How does that add up or subtract into living in dimensions and shit? Hell, I still have trouble with the times tables, so what do I know? Didn't matter none. Just wrote it off as part of the bill I had to pay to get that pussy. Let me tell you, in the sack, that name of hers wasn't just about teeth."

"Possible you liked being with her so much," I said, "that when she quit being with you and started skinning someone else's banana, you got jealous and did her in? That possible?"

"Don't be ridiculous. I loved that woman. Loved her like only an idiot could love her."

"Bet that's right," Leonard said.

Ace looked wounded.

Leonard said, "Where'd you get that hat?"

"What?"

"The hat. Where'd you get it?"

Ace told him.

"How much did it cost?"

Ace told him.

"That ain't bad," Leonard said.

12

I figured we had out of him all we were going to get, at least under the circumstances. Combined with the fact that we were all guilty of breaking and entering a home that didn't belong to any of us, even if the door was left unlocked, we decided to play it quiet and decamp.

We left out of the house, turning the inside lock behind us, so that when we closed the door it clicked solid shut. Ace stepped on ahead of us and was around the side of the house before we were.

As me and Leonard reached the walk, the black cat came out from between the shrubs, where perhaps it had still been shitting, and crossed in front of us.

"Oh, good, that's par for the course," Leonard said. "Black cat crosses our path."

When we got in the car, I saw in the rearview mirror that Ace was climbing into a junky black truck parked across the street and back from us. Leonard turned and wrote its license plate down on a notepad for good measure.

No one seemed to be watching us besides Ace. There was no one out in the yards or peeking through house windows. No spy drones buzzed overhead, and there were no street cameras. Ace didn't drive by us shooting a tommy gun.

As we cruised away from there, I said to Leonard, "What do you think?"

"I think everybody's lying."

"Maybe Ace was lying a little," I said, "but I don't think he was lying a lot."

"You seem in the mood to believe everybody. Let me sell you a sack of shit, 'cause in the morning it's going to turn into a bag of gold."

We found a dollar store where I could get something for my chair-induced headache, and then we drove to the Mexican restaurant on the block next to the bookstore and ate. They served damn good chili there and I took my headache cure with a glass of iced tea.

After we ate, I decided to let Jackrabbit stay missing a few minutes more, having by this point concluded she had split the country or was lying dead in a ditch somewhere and was not all that worried about our timing or anyone else's. I didn't have good feelings about the baby either.

We went to the used-book store and prowled around for a few minutes while I waited for the headache medicine to kick in.

Leonard bought some Western novels and I bought a book by a guy named Rocky Hawkins. It was *He Ain't Heavy, He's My Brother: Guns, Girls and Gambling in East Texas,* a memoir. It was about growing up in East Texas, and it looked interesting. His father had been a gangster.

The day had mostly eased away from us by that time, and

frankly we didn't know what else to do outside of finding George, and to be honest, my headache was so bad by then I wasn't up to it. Leonard drove my car while I closed my eyes and nursed my pain. He hauled us out of Marvel Creek to the nearby city of Longview where we could find a hotel.

We ended up in one that sat near the highway and was as big and soulless as an abandoned aircraft hangar. We got a room on the second floor overlooking the highway. I took my headache medicine again and went to look in the bathroom mirror at where the chair had hit me. A knot had come up that was no bigger than a cantaloupe, and my skin had turned bruise-blue.

I stripped down to my underwear and lay down on my bed, and Leonard lay on his bed with his head propped up with pillows and read. I wasn't up to reading. I thought I'd shut my eyes for a moment, but when I woke up I'd been asleep for a lot more than a moment. It had been hours. I had dreamed of Sebastian having his stomach cut open while he was alive, his hands stuck deep in his pockets, steam rising up from his belly as his innards were exposed to the air. He was smiling and his teeth were covered with blood.

By this time, it was dead dark and the air-conditioning was constantly cutting on and off. Leonard lay on his bed with his hands behind his head. I could tell he was awake, lying in the dark, thinking.

I still felt bad and decided I might as well stay in bed, but I had a hard time getting back to sleep. I would close my eyes and lie there awhile, and then the air conditioner would act up again, and once I sort of got used to that, a rainstorm came through with a sound like an army dragging chains. The lightning cracked and the thunder pealed; the wind that pushed it coiled around the hotel like an invisible constrictor.

I sat up and saw Leonard sitting on the edge of his bed, looking out the window. The curtains were pulled back and he was watching lightning stitch across the sky. When the thunder rolled, the hotel shook. The nightstand clock was flashing red bars instead of numbers. The electricity had been off for a bit.

I went over and sat on the side of Leonard's bed, said, "Pretty big storm."

"Yep. Makes you feel small. Head any better?"

"A little. That son of a bitch could swing a chair."

We watched the lightning some more, listened to the rain come down in jagged sheets, fade away, and come back hard again. I got up and stood by the window, looked out at the highway. I liked the way the rain hit it and the way the streetlights rippled in the water and the way headlights wavered on the concrete when cars came along. I liked how the tires splashed through the streaming rain and the droplets rose up and the light filled them so that they looked momentarily like molten beads of gold.

Leonard got up and stood by me. "I like to pretend it's washing away all the bad shit in the world. Sometimes, when the thunder isn't too loud, and there's just the rain and no lightning, I lay down thinking that way, and I can sleep better."

"Not a bad thing to imagine."

"Yeah, but when it stops, and I get up and go outside again, the same shit is there. I kind of hate everybody. Except you. And sometimes I'm not so sure about you."

13

We ate the free hotel breakfast and went to work.

The address for George was a junkyard on the outskirts of Marvel Creek. On the way there, we passed the ruins of the old drive-in theater where I had made love to girlfriends in the backseat of my car. Once monsters and cowboys, gangsters and such, had roamed across those screens, but now those days were gone, and it made me a little sad.

The junkyard was almost to the top of a large red-clay hill that looked as bleak as an Orc's wet dream, the junkyard cars resembling the husks of ravaged insects. Some were in rows, and some were in heaps, and there were platters of metal that had once been cars in stacks, like fat pancakes.

There was a greasy white sign pinned against a tin privacy fence that said GEORGE'S JUNKYARD, and there was a gap in the fence where the chain-link gate was open. We coasted through and got out. Somewhere inside, a dog was barking. There was a lot of bass in that bark.

A whining and metal screeching noise led us to a large man sitting high up in a car crusher's saddle, working the levers, smashing up an old Dodge truck, turning it from a truck into one of the large metal pancakes. I recognized him from his photo with Jackie, the one Judith had shown us. It was George. He had weathered a lot since the photo, like life had held him down and slapped him, but he was still easy to recognize. In person, he had a threatening air about him, like a thunderstorm building on the horizon.

Nearby, on a chain big enough for tugboat use, was a squatting, blue-skinned, scarred-looking pit bull. The chain was about ten feet long and was attached to a big dog house. The dog was barking nonstop, just in case we might not have noticed him.

George saw us, looked at us with an expression akin to an eagle considering swooping down on a couple of mice. He killed the machine and hoisted himself down. He looked bigger on the ground, bigger than Ace. Certainly bigger than either of us.

"Yeah," he said.

"You George?" I said.

I knew he was, of course.

I stuck out my hand. George glanced at it but didn't shake it. I dropped it to my side. Leonard was looking at the dog.

"He don't like black people," George said.

Leonard walked over to the dog.

"Better get away from there," George said. "He'll tear your ass up."

Leonard squatted, started speaking in a soothing manner. The dog kept barking. He was showing his teeth and the teeth were foam-flecked.

"He's gonna eat that nigger," George said.

"Might want to come back, Leonard," I said.

Leonard eased his hand closer, palm down, kept talking softly. "It's okay, boy. It's all right. I'm a friend."

"Gonna tear your arm off, nigger," George said.

"You and me will talk in a moment," Leonard said. He eased his hand toward the dog some more. The dog quit barking. "Good boy."

The dog lunged, snapped at Leonard's hand, but Leonard moved it just in time.

"Told you," said George. "Rex will get you good."

Leonard tried again, continuing with the soothing talk. "Rex. It's all right."

The dog sat down.

I saw George's face grow even more rigid than it already was.

Leonard patted the dog on the head and the dog let him.

"Goddamn it," George said. "Rex has gone to seed."

"No," Leonard said. "He's tired of being on a chain."

"I let him loose at night in the yard to discourage light-fingered visitors."

"But there's no one here then, is there?" Leonard said. "He gets lonely." Leonard was hugging the dog's neck now.

"Get away from my dog."

Leonard took his time, patted the dog some more, then came over to stand where me and George stood.

"You got a way with dogs," George said.

"Yeah, it's people I don't like. Ought not keep him chained up like that," Leonard said.

"Who are you two? Fucking ASPCA? You come here to give me freelance dog advice, or you got a real reason for being here? Buy some junk or take a hike. I got cars to crush."

I knew Leonard, and I knew he had not dismissed that whole "nigger" business, but as of late, he seemed to be a little calmer. These days he was more likely to cripple you than kill you. But it could be a passing phase.

A man about my height and build but ten to fifteen years younger came out from behind the crusher. He was a nice-looking man with dark brown, cut-close hair and a face as smoothly shaved as a model's pussy. He was wearing a crisp bright smile that looked only a little less sincere than the one they paint on ventriloquist dummies. He had on a black T-shirt and black slacks and shoes to match. His nose appeared to have been broken at one time, giving his face a look of both boyish geniality and rakish menace.

"What's up?" he said. He said that like he had sensed a disturbance in the force, à la *Star Wars,* and was trying to calm it.

"Couple of dog lovers have come to visit Rex," George said.

Leonard still had his eyes locked on George. He seemed to have hardly noticed the other man, but I knew better. One he was trying to intimidate, and the other he was watching without seeming to. There was this thing about the man in the black T-shirt that made you think he wanted you to notice him, and I think that's why Leonard wasn't.

"Ah," the man in black said. "Yes, and I hope you have asked him to give the dog more priority, something better than a short chain and a long life to live on it. I have suggested it, but so far, no response."

"Who says Rex gets a long life," George said. "Hell, he's happy. He's a dog. He gets to fight other dogs from time to time, and he hasn't lost yet. He likes that. That, and eating and fucking and cat-killing, that's his pleasure."

"You fight dogs?" Leonard said.

"When the law doesn't catch me," George said. He smiled. He was missing a top back tooth. I hoped it had been knocked out with a two-by-four. I know Leonard was considering knocking the rest out with his fists, and it had certainly crossed my mind. Dog-fighting is next to child abuse in my book.

"Horrid business," the other man said. "They call me Professor." He came forward and shook our hands. "George here, he's a friend, and he's all right, but he's not, shall we say, refined."

"Oh, hell, Professor," George said.

That's when I noticed two men drifting out from a row of cars and moving in our direction. They were dressed alike in clothes that looked too heavy for the climate. Long-sleeved white shirts and black vests that I knew were designed to cover holstered guns. They had thick hair that was black as death combed tight against their heads, and whatever they used to hold it in place glimmered in the sunlight like a waxed car. They were both tall and lean, alabaster faces and thick lips, and the same features. Twins. They came over and stood by George, and I have to tell you, I have never seen deader faces than those, eyes as black and empty as tunnels to nowhere.

Professor said, "Oh, that's the Fairview twins. They work for me, but I won't introduce you to them. They don't make friends all that well."

"They don't look to me like they could make change," Leonard said. He was studying them like they were specimens in a petri dish.

The twins seemed not to blink, and now they were no longer moving.

I turned my attention to George, said, "What we're here for is

70

we're looking for Jackie Mulhaney, sometimes known as Jackrab-bit. You know her, don't you?"

"Knew her," George said. "Bitch was crazy. Always going on about numbers and dimensions or some such shit. Ran around with the wrong kind of people. I finally had enough of her. I've al-ready had enough of you, for that matter. I don't know you from a sack of rocks, coming in here fucking with my dog."

"Be friendly," Professor said.

"You don't make them be friendly," George said, nodding at the twins.

"They are something else," Professor said. "You run a business."

"Not like they want any of this business," George said, nodding at us this time. "I think they're giving me the business, that's what I think."

"Answer their questions, George," Professor said. "Go on."

"You said she was running with the wrong kind of people," I said. "What do you mean by 'wrong kind of people'?"

"Ran around with people outside her place in life," George said. "She took a step down."

"You mean she was hanging with the brothers, huh?" Leonard said.

"Ain't my brothers."

"Reason she changed up like that is the dicks," Leonard said. "We black men all got enormous dicks. Mine is so big and heavy I keep it in the car."

"You're not all that funny," George said.

"Hey," Leonard said. "Who's joking."

Professor chuckled a little, but it didn't sound all that sincere to me. The twins hadn't so much as moved.

"I've talked all I'm going to talk, coming in here telling me how to raise my dog, asking me questions ain't none of your business. Ought to bust your heads."

Leonard smiled, but there was nothing friendly about it.

"I think you only think you're bad," Leonard said. "Pushing us around, that won't be like shoving some cracker that owes you money, chaining up some trusting dog. It might take a little more work. You might need an overnight bag. And I hope you got room up your ass for them twins, 'cause that's where I'm going to shove them."

George moved forward slightly. Leonard didn't move at all. Neither did the twins.

"Here now, George," Professor said, and he touched George on the shoulder.

George glared at Leonard, but he had stopped moving.

"Get out of my junkyard," George said.

"All right," I said.

The twins finally moved. Almost in unison they slipped dark sunglasses from their pockets and put them on. That was it. When they had them on, they let their hands hang by their sides again.

"Let me walk you gentlemen out," Professor said. He looked back at the twins and George. "I'll be fine. Stay here."

"Where'd you get the bookends?" Leonard said, nodding at the twins.

"Best not to antagonize them," Professor said.

Leonard stared at them a little longer, then we turned and started out, Professor walking with us.

As we went, Professor said, "George isn't really a bad man, just a little unrefined."

"That so?" Leonard said.

When we got to the car Professor said, "Let me explain it as best I can, keeping it brief. Once there were a lot of folks in this part of the country that felt they were superior to people that weren't like them."

"You mean people who weren't white?" Leonard said.

"Correct," Professor said, and nodded. "They were pretty foolish about the idea. Hated people with darker skin, led to them doing some very nasty things to them. Lynching, for example. It was our way or the highway. That was the white view."

"I remember it unfondly," Leonard said.

"I suppose so," Professor said. "Me, I'm not like that. I'm not filled with that kind of hate. But I am a segregationist. Not a racist."

"Segregationist is just another way to spell racist," Leonard said. "Only difference is the long word wears a hat and tie."

"No," Professor said. "There is a difference. I can talk to you and work with you and generally get along with you, but I believe the races are supposed to be separated. I think it's God's word and nature's law. You over there, me over here. We can see each other on the street, can speak, even call ourselves friends, but when we part ways, you go to where you belong, and I go to where I belong. I believe Negroes should have their own section, if you will."

"Nigger Town," Leonard said.

"You said it, I didn't. I try not to use that word. I know it's offensive, but I don't believe in the absolute mixing of the races and certainly not dating and marrying. You come to my house, that's my castle. I might ask you in. I might give you a cup of coffee and not do what they did of old, which was break the cup after you drank out of it."

"Wow, you are just a beacon of contemporary thinking," Leonard said.

Professor didn't blink, just plowed ahead.

"You work for me or I know you, Negro or not, you got your-self in trouble, I'd be there to bail you out, help you out. Up to a point."

"You're assuming black people get in trouble on a regular ba-sis?" I said.

"Not at all. I think there are good and bad on both sides of the fence. I merely believe in a fence with a gate, so we can cross over to either side for certain things, work, a bit of this, a bit of that, but I think sometimes we need to lock that gate. I wouldn't want the sun to go down with a black person in the house, nor, on the other hand, do I believe you should want a white person to be in yours. The mixing of races is not intended, and that is why we have different colors of skin. Tribal identification. It's a natural law, if not currently a legal one. Some believe we can't change that, can't have separate but equal, but I think we can, and will. We have to return to a more balanced life. Bar the Hispanics from crossing the border. Put up a wall. Keep other religions and races out of America. Our country can only hold so many comfortably. That's common sense. Is that racist?"

"I'm going to go with the idea that it is," I said. "Leonard lived at our house. Never ended up missing one piece of silverware while he was there. Vanilla cookies, however, you have to watch out for. Comes to those, he's without a conscience."

"They call my name," Leonard said.

"You can do as you please," Professor said. "But I believe there is a place for us all, and—"

"Is this where you talk about each kind of bird knows its place and doesn't mate with the other?"

"Perhaps," Professor said.

"What about dogs and wolves, donkeys and horses?" Leonard said. He looked at me. "Will a squirrel fuck a rabbit, Hap?"

"I think they have trouble catching them," I said.

Professor let a sagging grin hang on his face. I liked that grin only a little better than the ventriloquist-dummy version.

"And I don't use that kind of language. That's what's wrong with the world today. Not enough standards. I think we need to return to standards, courtesy, decent language, and a kind separation of races."

"You talk about keeping people in their place due to race, but you're worried about someone saying 'fuck'?" I said.

"Forget it," Professor said. "This will go nowhere."

"I got a question for you," Leonard said. "What you doing here with George at the junkyard? You work here?"

"I'm sort of an adviser," Professor said. "I was up at his house getting a drink, saw you fellows. I sometimes use the forklift to poke cars into the crusher for him. I enjoy the work."

"Do the twins hold your coat while you do that?" Leonard asked.

"If I want them to, but I'm not wearing a coat."

"In hot weather, maybe they sweat for you," Leonard said.

"If I ask them to."

"On what do you advise?" I said.

"Race relations, you might say."

"You need an adviser for that?" Leonard said.

"Also, I own a piece of the junkyard. Own a piece of a number of businesses in town. Completely own some of them. I make my living through investments. I advise on how to run successful businesses, here and elsewhere. I try to lay out nonviolent plans for a return to segregation. If I own a place, or a part of it, I have more power and can make recommendations."

"Like separate water fountains," I said.

"Heavens, no," Professor said. "That's ridiculous. Recommendations on how to actually live apart in harmony."

"Now that we've got your philosophy, can we ask you something else?" I said.

"Of course," he said. He was so congenial I wanted to punch him in the mouth.

"What did you know of Jackie Mulhaney, also called Jackrabbit?"

"She was with George for a while," Professor said. "He found it uncomfortable that she crossed racial lines, as he should. She was all right, though. Beautiful woman. But he did the right thing. As I said, there have to be boundaries. She was too smart for him as well. Is that all, gentlemen?"

I nodded. "Suppose it is."

"You have quite a knot on your head there, Mr. Collins."

"I do indeed," I said.

"Might want to put some ice on that," he said, then turned and walked briskly in the direction of the crushing machine, which we could hear hungrily munching on cars, making them squeak and scream.

76

14

Professor creeped me out more than George," I said.

"I hear that," Leonard said. "It's just the same old thing wearing a clean set of clothes, speaking in a polite voice. Guy like that, he's got more of an agenda than he's letting on."

"I have a feeling, you scratch Professor deep enough, you get George."

"And you send George to school and give him a haircut and a good bath, you get Professor, provided George could work his way through third grade first."

"Yep," I said. "Professor has got this insane mission to go back in time to Jim Crow days."

"Like I said last night, Hap. Just when you think the river is flowing nice and clean, along comes the sewage. I still believe in the American dream, but I also got to admit that the honey has a lot of flies on it."

"You can pick out the flies if you got the patience."

"I don't have it. And how about those fucking twins, man? They really creeped me out."

"They're like the walking dead," I said.

"But they ain't got as good a personality."

While I drove, Leonard called our buddy Chief Marvin Hanson in LaBorde, gave him Ace's license plate, asked him if he could run it for us, find a home location.

Leonard got off the phone, said, "He's going to do it, hit us back later. Said he had real police work to do first. How dare he?"

"Very rude," I said.

I looked in my rearview mirror. There was a black pickup behind us. For a moment, I thought it was Ace, but it was a truck in far better condition.

"You know," I said, "that pickup started following us pretty quick after we left the junkyard. I thought it might be coincidence, but I'm beginning to wonder."

"Do some turns," Leonard said.

I took a side road, then another, cruised through a neighborhood of old but nice houses, took another turn, hit Main Street, and drove down it all the way out to the Sabine River Bridge in the direction of Tyler.

The truck stayed with us.

I drove over the bridge and kept going, right on out of Marvel Creek. The truck crossed the bridge behind us, but when I looked in my rearview mirror, it was turning around.

"I think we were just ran out of town," I said.

"No, we left of our own free will. Separate but equal. I'm going to draw a line between these seats, Hap. You stay over there, and I'll stay over here."

"It's my car. You'll walk."

"Yeah, massa, I done forgot that. Maybe I shine yo' shoes or lick yo' ass, Massa Hap, and won't be no need to set me 'side the road."

"We'll see how you act," I said.

"You know how I might act?"

"How?"

"Spending about twenty minutes kicking your ass up under your ears."

"Better bring yourself a picnic lunch and a thermos of coffee, 'cause it's going to take you more than twenty minutes."

"Shit, all I got to do is hit you with a chair."

"Don't mention a chair," I said. "The word makes my head hurt."

15

Leonard's cell rang.

"Yeah. Sure. Let me write that down."

He got his pad and pen and scribbled.

"Thanks. We owe you one. Yeah. You're right. We've kind of got a long list of owes. Catch up to you later."

"Marvin, I assume."

"Yeah. I got Ace's address, his place of work too."

"That was actually pretty quick," I said.

"Technology," Leonard said. "Next thing is we're going to have cameras up our ass."

"They call that a colonoscopy, and that wouldn't be a recording I'd like to see," I said. "We got nothing more to say to Ace right now, though, do we?"

"Guess not, but let's locate Ace's crib in case we need that information for later, see where he works."

This meant we had to go back to the far side of Marvel Creek. I turned the car around and crossed the bridge again.

We found his house on a dirt road with three or four other houses nearby. The house was small and weathered and looked about three years from needing to be held up with a sturdy stick. It looked like some places Leonard and I had lived in once upon a time. These days we were more prosperous.

We didn't try to visit. Figured he was at work anyway, and right then we had nothing new to ask, but knowing where he hung out seemed like something we might need later.

As we drove away, I realized the black pickup was with us again. It had probably joined us not long after we came back through Marvel Creek on our way to locate Ace's house. I had been so focused on the address, I hadn't noticed it right away.

I told Leonard they were back.

"I'm tired of this shit," Leonard said.

He opened the glove box and got out the little automatic I kept in there. It was small caliber and could probably knock over a cardboard target if a high wind was helping.

We were still out in the country and were now far away from the little grouping of houses. There was only the blacktop road we were on and the trees on either side of it. We did pass a pasture with a few cows in it. None of them waved.

"Pull it over, and let's get this done with," Leonard said.

"Might be best to wait until we're around more people," I said. "They might be less inclined to shoot us."

"I don't give a shit, pull over."

I gave a shit, but I pulled over. Truth to tell, I was tired of them too.

I found a spread of gravel beside the road that had a concrete picnic table with benches attached, and next to it was a historical marker. I pulled over and got out, and so did Leonard.

I reached back inside the car and took a sawed-off ball bat out from under the front seat, held it against my leg, and walked to the back of my car. Leonard had the little handgun in his front pocket, his shirttail over it.

The two guys got out. They were big guys. One was a little fat and walked with a limp, held his head to one side. He had scraggly brown hair and a scragglier mustache. He came toward me carrying an ax handle, and then he slowed down, and a smile cut across his face.

"Hap Collins, you old fucker," he said.

"Jimmy Hems," I said.

"You remember Lou here, don't you?" he said, and he jerked a thumb at his companion.

Lou looked a lot like Jimmy, only not as fat and minus the limp and the head held to one side. They both had the same hair-and-mustache stylist. Lou was Jimmy's younger brother.

"Hi, Lou," I said.

Lou nodded.

"You lose the head goes on that ax handle?" I said to Jimmy.

"Naw, not at all." He tossed the ax handle to the side of the road. "Lou, pack your shit up."

That's when I saw Lou had brass knuckles on his fists. He took them off and put one set in his right pants pocket, the other set in his left.

"What the fuck is this?" Leonard said.

"You don't remember me, do you, Leonard?" Jimmy said.

"Nope."

"You whipped my ass down by the river once at a tire-fire fight."

"Remember the fights, don't remember you," Leonard said.

"You knocked me out."

82

"I've knocked a lot of people out," Leonard said.

Jimmy smiled at Leonard, turned to me. "Listen here, Hap. I got this problem, and I think we ought to discuss it."

"I'm not a psychiatrist, Jimmy," I said. "Even a town like Marvel Creek might have a therapist in it. You could maybe trade some chickens for therapy. Didn't your family used to raise them?"

"I'm all out of chickens, Hap. Look, let's cut the cute shit. Let's talk."

"Where?" I said. "Coffee shop?"

"Picnic table seems private enough," he said.

Jimmy and Lou were nearer the back of my car now, having come up on little cat feet, like the poet said. They were standing a couple of yards from us. Leonard and I were leaning against the trunk of my car. Leonard had his hand in his pocket. I held my friend the sawed-off ball bat in front of me, the heavy end resting in the palm of one hand. I patted it now and again, just as a reminder.

"You remember that time at the Dairy Bob when Bob run them fellows out of there for acting fools, and they set a car on fire out back, thought it was Bob's?" Jimmy said.

"I do. Burned down their own cousin's car instead, as I recall. He had a car similar to Bob's and had parked there while he and some friends went riding around in someone else's car. If I could remember who all was in that car, or was supposed to be, it would take a real burden off of me, Jimmy."

"I know, doesn't matter," Jimmy said. "You remember the cousin who owned the car, Taylor Atkins?"

"A little," I said. "Thought it didn't matter."

"Taylor found out it was his cousins done it, burned it down to the fucking frame, and he and some of his buddies took his cousins down to the river bottoms and beat the dog shit out of 'em."

"I remember the story," I said.

"Taylor was close to his cousins, more like brothers, but he didn't have money to replace his car, so he had to have some satisfaction out of it, even if what they did was an accident, mistaken car identity. Main one involved with starting the fire, Phil, you remember Phil Atkins? Well, he lost an eye over that. I think Taylor hit him with a plank or something."

"I heard a bottle."

"Whatever, an eye was lost. They were a year out of high school, still hanging around Marvel Creek, scraping by, and you know what? They'd still be here if it weren't for prison. They live there now. They got a comfortable regimen. Taylor killed somebody, and the rest of them are in for this and that. All of the cousins, two or three of the friends. They got some serious stretches to do, and Taylor won't be coming out under his own power."

"You seem to have lost the point to your story," I said. "If there was one."

"So, Phil loses an eye, and it wasn't personal," Jimmy said.

"The hell it wasn't," I said.

"Okay. It was personal in that the cousins couldn't pay for the car, but they were still cousins, and they went on and got along together after that, even married sisters. Not their own, but another family with sisters. They're divorced now, and of course, the cousins are all in the hoosegow."

"Listen, Jimmy," I said, "you got some moral to this story you're trying to get across, I kind of wish it would show up. I'm starting to feel the effects of old age here."

"You and me, we were friends in high school—"

"We knew each other," I said. "We got along because we didn't know each other enough not to get along."

"That's right. We got along. Well, the cousins got along too, but there had to be retribution for that car, and it was a point of honor, even if in the end, all was forgiven."

"Is this shoe ever going to drop?" Leonard said.

"What I'm saying is Taylor didn't want to do what he did, but he had to make sure he kept his honor intact. That's what it was all about. What we got here isn't exactly the same situation, but it's something like it. We got hired to follow you, didn't we, Lou?"

Lou nodded.

"We are supposed to see that you leave town and help you leave if you don't choose to do it on your own. Thought you were gone for a bit there, and nothing needed doing, and I was happy about that, and then damn if you didn't come back. Saw you again, followed you out here, and now, here we are."

"Yep, here we are."

"Wait a minute," Leonard said. "So that story you told is a kind of fucking parable about you doing the honorable thing, keeping your word, but you don't have to if we leave? My suggestion to you is work up another story that's more on point. But what I'm getting here from that fucked-up story, and believe me, it's like a crow sorting through cow shit to find a corn kernel, you're saying you been hired by someone to check us up and light us up if need be. Could the asshole hired you be George, or Professor Asshole?"

"Professor," Jimmy said. "Pays good wages for little jobs. It's a living."

"Let's sit at the picnic table," I said. "Your story kind of wore me out."

Jimmy said, "I got some beer in a cooler of ice in the back of the truck. Want one?"

"No, thanks," I said.

"I'll have one," Leonard said.

"Lou, get this man a beer."

"I'll walk with you, just in case one of the beers shoots bullets," Leonard said.

When Leonard and Lou came back, Leonard was carrying a beer. Lou was carrying two. I could see water dripping off their hands from reaching into the cooler. Lou gave Jimmy a beer, kept one for himself.

I put the shortened ball bat on the back of the car trunk and we all walked over to the picnic table and sat down, but before Leonard sat, he took the gun out of his pocket and laid it on the table next to his beer.

"Do you need that?" Jimmy said.

"I don't know yet," Leonard said.

The rain of the night before had left dampness in the trees, and being close to them we could feel the humidity. The heat oozed out of the greenery and made us sticky as sugar doughnuts. A light, almost transparent mist floated a few inches above a run of water near the trees, and the mist clung between the trees like a fallen cloud. I could see insects wiggling in the water.

"I want you to understand, fellows, that I don't cotton to Professor's beliefs," Jimmy said. "I cotton to his money. Lou here, he's on the fence."

Lou nodded.

"Has he got something in his throat?" I said.

"Ah, that's right. You didn't really know Lou."

"I didn't really know you," I said.

"Lou doesn't talk much," Jimmy said. "Bottom line is this. I don't care one way or the other what the truth is, what someone's beliefs are, if I'm getting paid to do a thing. And I'm getting paid."

"Does your job have to come with a lecture?" I said. "Because I'm starting to get bored."

"Always a smart mouth," Jimmy said. "Even in school."

"How would you know?" I said. "We didn't hang."

"Reputation, Hap, reputation. You had one. But listen here, man. I'm trying to reach what we might call a goddamn fucking compromise, and I'm trying to get there for your own good, the both of you, and maybe mine and Lou's good. Shit can go sideways for any of us, so I want to avoid conflict."

"That's big of you," Leonard said.

"Professor, he's a solid sort, just has some, well, how do we say it, old-style beliefs in a fresh package. I don't know how much he believes his own bullshit or how much he's just playing to a certain type, but the thing is, from time to time he needs someone to help him out on certain matters. And the matter he wants help with is he wants you and Leonard to leave town."

"Does his wanting us to leave have anything to do with Jackie Mulhaney?" I asked.

"It may, it might not. I didn't ask. Don't care."

"Did you know Jackie?"

"Who didn't? She was pretty wild, and maybe a little crazy. But beyond that, I know very little, like she had been with George, and this black guy . . . can't remember his name."

Lou said, "Ace."

"Damn," Leonard said. "He speaks."

Lou smiled like a baby that had just passed gas.

"Professor kind of liked her, I think," Jimmy said. "Thought she was hot enough to burn down a barn. Said as much. But thing is, I don't care if Professor is fucking a duck on Wednesdays and a pig on Thursdays. I don't want to do something bad to you two, and that's why I seek a compromise. Just leave town."

"I was thinking," Leonard said, "we might do something bad to you two."

"Leave, don't come back," Jimmy said. "I don't want to get rough. I hate that kind of business, but it's the business we got. We're willing to give you until tomorrow morning. And that's stretching it. But we see you in town again after that, we got to, you know, make plans for you to leave. I should also ask, do you remember my brother Delf?"

"He was in my grade," I said.

"He's police chief here," Jimmy said. "Just so you know. Have I made my position clear?"

"I think so," I said.

"Next time, we'll be a little more vigorous."

"Don't think we haven't got some vigor ourselves," Leonard said.

"Oh, I know you do. This is merely a polite warning and a desire for it not to go any farther. It was the twins, and I understand you met them, because if you met Professor, you met them, they aren't as affable as we are, and I'll tell you, frankly, they scare me a little."

"It's us you ought to be afraid of," Leonard said.

"I admit a bit of nervousness about tangling with you two, and that's another reason I'd rather avoid it. But I'm nervous, not afraid. Lou here, I don't think he's given it much thought."

"Yeah," Leonard said. "He don't look like he's thinking about much."

Lou smiled.

"But Professor calls out the twins, all discussion is off. I'm giving you a chance here to go your way. I mean, really, does finding a woman you don't even know mean that much to you?"

"We got honor too," I said. "We gave our word."

Jimmy nodded. I thought he sincerely looked a little sad.

"Think we'll head out now. Remember that time line."

"Remember I already whipped you once," Leonard said. "Meant so little to me, I'd forgotten it until you mentioned it, and frankly, I still don't remember you but I'm glad I did it."

Jimmy smiled a smile that made him look a lot more like Lou.

They got up from the table.

"Jimmy," I said. "One thing I have to ask, man: What the fuck happened to your neck?"

It was a mean thing to ask, but I was feeling mean right then.

"Car accident," Jimmy said. "Some kind of misalignment when it healed. But don't think that has any effect on how I get things done. Been nice seeing you boys. Just don't let me see you after tomorrow morning."

"Yeah, well, keep your head up," Leonard said.

Jimmy snorted, then he and Lou walked back to the pickup, got in it, and drove off.

16

I cruised us slowly back into town, and rolling back in, the bad things that had happened here when I was younger came down on me fat and heavy. Memory has weight.

To lift the weight, I thought about a time here when it had not been all bad, back when I practically lived in the woods, along the creeks and along the river, back when I would fish and the world seemed all right, and I believed in the code of the Lone Ranger, about how good always won over bad, and that things were constantly set straight by honor and daylight.

I remembered the fishing hole that was just off the Sabine River, where the water ran in and filled it, and willows grew thick all around it. It was deep there, though the hole was not wide. You could easily throw a rock across it. You could drop a line in the water and always catch a fish, always have your dinner. The sky was wonderful to see through the limbs and leaves of the trees that shaded the hole, especially as the day died and the night rose up, and the sky turned a strange purple because of the way the sunlight bled through the trees. Then there was the night, and the night wasn't bad either, because it seemed soft, and there were the stars to be seen between the limbs and leaves, and the crickets would make their sounds, and the bullfrogs theirs. If it was a moonlit night, it was like traveling by spaceship, lying there on the banks of the blue hole on a blanket, heading into the moonlight, hating to walk back to the car carrying my gear, hating to go away from there, trying to hold on to that moment forever.

I was musing on that when Leonard said, "That beer was like horse piss. Got to think Lou picked it out at the store, must have been some kind of bargain shit. Oh, hell, think he poisoned me?"

"It was sealed," I said. "No. He didn't poison you. Stuff Jimmy said about his older brother, Delf, being police chief, that was a way of telling us they could kill us and no one would look for us even if we were lying on the steps of the Marvel Creek Police Department wearing tutus. Only thing is, I remember Delf as an all-right guy. Kind of a blowhard, but all right."

"Maybe he's had a hangnail or two since then and it's turned him bitter."

"That's possible. And Jimmy, what I remember of him, he seemed all right too."

"He's not all right, Hap. Neither is his goofy brother. One thing for sure, we've somehow stirred the soup."

"Always do," I said.

"Question is, what have we stirred up? Came here asking about Jackrabbit, and we meet a preacher who liked her, find out her father was a weird masochist, next you get hit by a chair and have to be rescued by me."

"That's how you saw it?"

"Yep. Then George threatens us, and we meet a very nice man

called the Professor who thought Jackie was pretty hot, but he doesn't like birds trying to mix. He introduces us to the twins, who also seemed very nice, and then he threatens us in a quiet way, and then he sends two goons to warn us to be out of town by tomorrow morning. It's been a big day."

"It has."

"And for the record, I don't cotton to threats from anyone," Leonard said.

"I, on the other hand, might be a little more prone to cotton a little, at least until I figure out why we're being threatened. Is this about Jackie or is it about black and white relations, and exactly why have we become the target for an ass whipping when we're merely asking about a missing lady who turns out to be good at math and is a little kooky?"

"Always the questions, never the answers," Leonard said.

"Know what, I say we visit Delf and say howdy."

"What else we got to do?"

17

The police station was a large stone building that looked more suitable for a library.

Leonard pulled the automatic pistol out from under his shirt, returned it to the glove box, and we went into the station like we owned it.

There was a pretty-faced plump lady at the desk. It was the kind of plumpness you wanted to roll in. Her cheeks were apple red and it didn't appear to be makeup. Her desk was behind a long glass wall with a little mouse-hole slot at the center bottom of it, and a metal fixture for speaking was positioned in the glass at mouth height.

She smiled at me, nodded at Leonard.

I stepped closer to the glass and put the smile on my face I used for seduction. It had worked at least twice in my lifetime.

"Can I help you, honey?" she said.

I missed really small towns right then, the casual sweetness they could have. "Honey" and "baby" and "child" and "sweetie" and so on. The sign on her desk said her name was Eula Jean Craig.

"You can," I said. "I'm wondering if the chief, Delf, is in. I'm an old classmate and wanted to say howdy, speak to him a minute."

"May I ask who's asking, sugar?" she said.

She was so unprofessional and sweet and sexy, I think I loved her a little. "Well, dear," I said, "tell him that an old classmate, Hap Collins, is here to see him, and I have a friend with me, Leonard Pine."

Eula Jean touched a button somewhere and there was a buzzing sound, and then "Yes, Eula," came a voice.

"Chief, there's a very nice-looking couple of gentlemen here would like to see you. One says his name is Hap Collins, and his friend is . . ." She leaned toward the metal fixture in the glass. "Sorry. What was it again?"

Leonard bent forward, said, "Leonard Pine."

She told the speaker that, and then we heard a voice say, "Well, send them back."

"That door is right there, gentlemen. And Hap, didn't you used to date my sister, Paulette?"

The last name clicked then. Paulette Craig.

"I did indeed."

"She's married now and has four kids, but I'm available."

"It's a lovely thought," I said, "but I'm with someone, and frankly, I'm too old for you."

"Oh, honey, don't let that scare you. If you die, you die." She grinned and pointed at the door, said, "I'll buzz you in."

We went through the door, and it led into a tiled hallway that looked as if it had just been polished by the heavenly angels.

Delf stepped out of a door and into the hallway. He had gained weight and his belly strained his shirt and made it gap in a spot, and that made his white T-shirt visible underneath his uniform. He had lost all his hair except for a graying ring around his head, but he had all his teeth and was smiling them at us.

"Damn, boy, I darn near forgot about you."

It was the kind of friendliness that comes with a certain amount of common history more than with true friendship.

"And Leonard, you might not know it," he said, "but I know you too."

"Say you do?" Leonard said.

We had walked up to him by then. He shook our hands and waved us into his office, which was as clean as the hallway.

He collapsed in a rolling chair behind his desk as if he were falling off the edge of a pier into deep water. He gestured at a couple of chairs arranged in front of the desk, and we sat down in those.

"You look just the same," he said, "except older, grayer, and heavier."

"Let me return that compliment," I said.

"And you, Leonard. I've heard of you. Word gets around, you know. I think you knocked my brother out once. You boys, you're kind of known as troubleshooters. Or is it troublemakers?"

"We're actually private detectives," I said.

"Whatever you are, word sure has got here, and some of it comes from my brother Jimmy."

"Ah," I said. "Native drums."

"Yeah, well, not drums. He called me a few minutes ago."

"Did he tell you he told us to get out of town by morning light?"

"No. Just said you had become a troublemaker, and he knew Leonard here, and he thought he was the same. Let me tell you something, Hap. Jimmy, he likes to think he has clout through me, and he's my brother, and I love him, Lou too, bless his dull little head, but the only clout I sling around is the law. Him telling me you're troublemakers, well, that remains to be seen, don't it? And if you're here to complain about him, you'll be getting in a long fucking line. But I promise you this. I'm going to uphold the law."

"That's good to hear," I said.

"How you like my receptionist?" he said. "You remember her sister? Dated her awhile, didn't you?"

"I did."

"She was a pretty one, and Eula out there, she is too. She might be packing more meat than she needs during a hot summer, but she's got it going on, don't she?"

"I agree."

"I'm fucking her, you know that?"

"It wasn't something she mentioned," I said. "She did kind of ask me out, though."

"I'm going to get her some sort of sign to wear that reads I'M FUCKING THE CHIEF, AND JUST THE CHIEF."

"It would clear matters up right away," I said.

He laughed at his own humor. I had a feeling if anything was going on between them, it wasn't true love, and maybe nothing was going on other than Delf trying to be his old blowhard, macho self.

"Did you agree to see us," Leonard said, "so you could tell us you're laying the pork to Chubby out there?"

I saw Delf's eyes darken a little, but then they cheered up equally fast.

"No. I agreed to see you because Hap and I went to school together."

"I'm not trying to fuck up y'alls reunion," Leonard said, "but

Hap actually came to see you for a purpose other than reminiscing."

"That right, Hap?"

"Complaining about your brothers was part of it," I said.

"Jimmy was trying to blow hot smoke up your ass, and then he tried to blow some up mine."

"A little of it might have got in the hole," I said. "Why I'm here, I took them seriously, and I'd rather not have to defend myself, because I might hurt someone."

"And I might kill someone," Leonard said.

"Are those threats?" Delf said.

"They're cautions," Leonard said.

"Break the law, either of you, and I'm coming after you. Same for my brothers. After Mama died, I didn't have much to do with them. You might remember my old man died back when I was in high school. Got cancer of the dick or some such, maybe it was the stomach or the liver. I don't know. But he got it, and it killed him."

I didn't remember, but I didn't say anything.

"Being the older brother, I raised them two best I could, played the father to them, tried to bring them up right, but it didn't stick. I became a cop, they became assholes. Jimmy, he's always blaming this or that for his station in life. He wouldn't have his neck leaning out to the side if he hadn't been drinking. Hit a deer one night, car went flying through the air. He didn't have his seat belt on, so he took a trip through the windshield. Surprisingly, it didn't cut him up as bad as you'd think, but it gave him that permanent nod after they got through fixing him up. Thought that might sober him, put him on another path, but nope. Kept walking between the briars, tangling up in them now and again. Hate to say it, but for Jimmy, and probably Lou, it's a matter of time."

"For the record," I said, "he was drinking and driving today."

"Noted. Not surprised."

"Got a question for you," Leonard said. "We're hired to find Jackie Mulhaney, called Jackrabbit. You got any way to help us on that?"

Delf put his feet on his desk, looked at the ceiling. "That crazy bitch. She had a dad crazier than her."

"You say that because of the way he died?" I said.

He removed his feet from the desk and let the chair settle.

"You know about that?"

"Heard from the preacher at the old theater," Leonard said.

"Damn good waste of a theater. And let me tell you something. I think that nice-talking preacher over there killed Sebastian to take over his church. Made up this fucked-up story about Sebastian wanting his guts put on his chest and some such. And by the way, that is how we found him. How would Jamesway know about that if he didn't do it?"

"He claims Sebastian tried to hire him to do it," I said. "But he turned him down."

"Didn't say shit about it until the body was found, then he tried to work his way out of being a suspect."

"Wouldn't have been a suspect had he not told that story," I said. "He could have just been quiet."

"I thought about that, but really. The guy wanted to suffer? Be cut open? Swallowed a key so it had to be cut out of him? Come on. And this ten-thousand-dollar shit. Where would he get that kind of money? Motherfucker probably had to wipe his ass on his shirttail because he couldn't afford toilet paper."

"I presume you looked in the bank vault?" I said.

"You know about that too? Well, isn't Jamesway the little chatterbox? I went to the bank and had them open Sebastian's box. Empty. Either there was never anything there, and Jamesway is lying through his sanctimonious teeth, or whoever killed Sebastian Mulhaney got the key and got the money. Then there's this whole thing with Jackrabbit. I think she and Jamesway worked this out together, did the deed, then she took half, he took half, and she took a hike. Or maybe even more likely, she's somewhere out in the woods, and she ain't there enjoying nature. She's part of it, courtesy of Church Boy."

"Yet you haven't arrested him," Leonard said.

Delf nodded. "Thinking something is true and proving it's true are two different things."

"You obviously knew Jackie," I said.

"Everyone in town did. She was a good-looking woman, in an odd kind of way. But there was something about her. My cop instincts tingled. I wouldn't have trusted that gal as far as I could throw her."

"Appreciate the information," I said.

"I didn't tell you a damn thing you didn't already know," Delf said. "You boys leaving town like my brother suggested? Not forcing you to, but I'd go if I was you. Jimmy and Lou aren't the only ones working for this fellow called Professor. My brothers don't give you trouble, others might."

"Like the twins," Leonard said.

"Like them. I tell you, those fuckers make my skin crawl. See them in the café, they just drink coffee. Never seen them eat, never heard them say a word. I think they live off coffee in the day, suck blood at night. I think they're Yankees."

"Got to be," Leonard said.

"Who are they?" I said.

"Professor calls them the Fairview twins."

"What he told us," Leonard said.

"But thing is, I haven't found any records on any twins named Fairview, so I doubt that's their name. I got nothing on them."

"What's Professor's story?" I said.

"I've pulled him in before for this and that. But nothing sticks. He's a pig farmer. Between here and Longview he's got a lot of land and a lot of pigs on it, raises them on concrete. Who the hell raises pigs on concrete?"

"Gonna guess he does," Leonard said.

"Got drains to wash away the pig shit. There's constant feeding. Makes a mint selling hogs and butchering hogs. Has a small packing plant of his own. Drive down the road that runs by it during the day, you can hear them hogs grunting and squealing. I heard him say when they're butchered, when they scream, it sounds like money. Professor owns all kinds of things, or at least has his finger in them. The café, gas stations, lots of property. He's got the money to get things done his way, and he's got the gift of gab."

"And George?" I asked.

"On paper George owns the junkyard, but he doesn't really. There's a kind of deal between him and Professor. He owes Professor for helping keep him afloat, orchestrating dogfights for him. This and that."

"Professor said he was against dogfights," I said.

"Only time he's against them is if the dog he's betting on loses," Delf said.

"Pit bull out there looks as if he's been chewed on a little," Leonard said.

"Don't think I condone that stuff, or fighting chickens either, but there's a whole bunch of those folks out and around here who do. Goes on no matter how much I try and stop it. They call it part of their culture, as if that makes it okay. Professor, he works under the table on a lot of things, out in the open on others. Dogfights, junkyards, the café. This and that. His idea is to buy up as much of the town as possible, control what he can't buy, and make this a haven for folks like himself. Thinks people of his ilk will flock here. Next thing is, they'll push me out and put in a puppet. Maybe even Jimmy. They'll have their own society, and believe me, it'll be lily-ass white. Truthfully, I don't know how much Professor believes his own bullshit, but if you talk it and promote it, even if your goal is power and money, far as I'm concerned, you believe it."

"In other words, he wants to run all the black people out to make a certain segment here happy," Leonard said.

"Mostly it's about immigrants these days."

"They're the new nigger," Leonard said.

"Oh, he hasn't forgotten the old hatreds. If there's a bell he can ring, a whistle he can blow, he does it. He's hitting heavy on anyone that doesn't fit the pattern he's cut. Pattern he knows will appeal to a lot of people. You know, I got a black police officer. Johnny Williams. Nice man, good cop. A friend. Couple of new recruits, also black. Hired them myself. Came from bigger cities, came with fine recommendations. Lots of experience. Next thing I plan to do is ease a woman in. Can you believe that? This day and time, and I have to ease a woman into a position, can't just go on and do it? Got some backwoods thinking here, guys."

"Sounds like you might have some of that concerning Eula," I said.

"Shit, me and Eula got our own program, and we handle it how we handle it. I may not get all the talk right, and I still like pussy and think about it and don't apologize for it, but I'm fair, boys. These officers I got, they moved here thinking it would be an easier lifestyle, but with Professor out there, those fucking twins, who we think are responsible for a lot of things that aren't good around here, well, my men, they got to be cautious every time they pull someone over for speeding. Lot of people think the Professor gave them a free pass to do as they please, long as who they do it to isn't white."

"Jimmy seemed apologetic about his current position," I said. "His heart didn't seem all in."

"Don't get fooled, Hap."

"What I tell him," Leonard said. "He's still thinking everyone is going to live in teepees and share each other's goods."

"Listen to your pal here," Delf said. "Don't underestimate Jimmy or the Professor, and watch out for Lou. He follows as close as shit on an ass hair when it comes to Jimmy. They're both like Mom said our old man was. 'People of opportunity,' she called them. And then Professor has others in his employment, and I don't mean the creepy twins. There's nothing solid on them, but there are rumors, some of them fairly sound and none of them about humanitarian deeds. Frankly, you might want to leave town. Not because you have to, not because I won't try and protect you, but because I might not be able to. Leonard here is just the sort that upsets Professor the most."

"He pretty much upsets everyone," I said.

18

I turned a corner and drifted us toward the café where we had eaten our breakfast and where we were planning on having lunch. The idea of going there had a new feel about it, knowing Professor had some ownership in it.

In the café, you got to choose where you wanted to sit, so we took a booth near the large plate-glass window at the front where we could see the street. The sky had turned as gray as an oyster shell, but what it contained was rain, not pearls. I figured within the next few hours the clouds would let the water loose.

The Coffee Spoon was a place where if you wanted to eat healthy you were shit out of luck. I feared even the salad might be deep-fried with a side of fried coffee.

I asked the waitress if they served omelets at lunch.

She was a sassy lady with a face tanned by cigarette smoke and framed by dark brown hair. You could see beauty had once been in that face, and when she turned a certain way, it pushed itself to the fore, and then it went away again. Once upon a time men most likely lined up around the block for her, but eventually, time had carried her out to sea and tried to drown her.

"Is it on the menu?" she said.

"No," I said.

"We don't have it."

"So nothing off the menu?"

"That's why we have a menu. Goddamn it. Are you Hap Collins?"

"I used to be," I said, "but lately I'm not so sure."

"Sharon Young. You remember me?"

I did. And in fact, men had indeed lined up for her attention. I had been one of them. I had been unsuccessful.

"Sorry," she said to Leonard. "What's your name, hon?"

"Leonard Wants a Cheeseburger," he said. "My friends call me Had a Cheeseburger."

She laughed. "Sure. I'll get to it."

But she didn't move, just smiled at me. She had good teeth, and when she smiled it caused wrinkles to appear at the edges of her eyes, but even still, that smile peeled ten years off her face. That light she had once had came back for a moment.

"I remember you in school," she said. "I had such a crush."

"On what?"

"You, silly."

"Really?"

"Yeah."

"I asked you out," I said. "I remember you, and I remember you said no."

"I was playing hard to get, way we were supposed to back then. Or way I thought we were supposed to. I thought you'd ask again. You didn't."

"I wanted to," I said.

"Isn't high school funny."

"I laugh every day, between the tears."

"I hear that. Best time of our lives. Bullshit. Come to think of it, though, for me, it might have been, and that's a sad statement. You doing okay?"

"I am."

"Wife?"

"Yep."

"Kids?"

"One girl."

"Me, I had three husbands and one got up one morning and said he was going to look for a job, tried to rob the bank that was across the street from where you fellows sit. They give out enchiladas now instead of loans."

"I know," I said. "We ate there last night. My first bank account was there. First State Bank. I'm assuming your husband's life of crime didn't turn out well."

"Everyone recognized him, of course. He hadn't thought about that problem. Andy Coleman, remember him?"

"Oh, hell. Really? Andy? You married Andy? Sorry, I'm just thinking—"

"Keep thinking it," she said, "he was a piece of"—she leaned in close to me—"shit. So, my John Dillinger tripped going down the steps prancing out to his getaway car. Dropped the money. Got up and ran off to his car without it, and then, know what? Car wouldn't start. Piece-of-crap Gremlin. Cops nabbed him, of course. Me and him got divorced while he was in prison. If he's getting any now, it's butt hole in cell block C. But to hell with all that. You want an omelet, I'll fix you an omelet. And you, Leon. What would you like?"

"Leonard," he said, "and still a cheeseburger, and double the onions and heap the fries."

"No, don't double the onions," I said. "I have to ride with him all day."

"Customer's always right, sugar," she said.

A redheaded man, tall and bony, wearing a khaki shirt and pants, guy who looked like you would imagine an oil-field worker would look, took a seat near the kitchen. Sharon noted his arrival.

"Back to work," she said. "Order coming up."

I watched her head to the kitchen. The girl she had once been moved under her waitress outfit, but there was more of her than before. I thought, Men are pigs, we really are, because that's the first thing I noticed, her being heavy, as if I had ever been a Greek god and had a right to judge.

She stopped at the booth near the kitchen, talked to the red-headed guy, wrote something on her pad, then went on about her business.

Later, when Sharon brought our food, I said, "Let me ask you a question, Sharon. Did you know a young woman named Jackie Mulhaney?"

"A little. Came in from time to time. Daddy was a weirdo that used to run the nut church that was once the picture show. Now some other nut runs it, but he's more pleasant. Me, I'm a Methodist."

"Dancing Baptist," Leonard said.

"That's the one," she said.

"Is there anything you can tell us about her?" I said.

Sharon thought a moment. "Not much that will amount to any-thing. Always had a salad with extra croutons. Had big teeth. Way men acted around her, I think those teeth must have looked good on her. Little horsy-looking, you ask me. I need to hit another lick. Got to look busy. Jobs don't get handed out in this town, especially the ones I'm good to do, and you need your coffee."

She went away for a moment, came back with a shiny coffeepot. She poured us coffee. I remembered that coffee from breakfast. It was still better than the Reverend Jamesway's coffee, but nothing so good you wanted a can of it.

"Know what she used to do?" Sharon said as she set the pot on the table. "She'd come in, bring her laptop, sit in that booth over there, on the side against the wall. That way she could type on her laptop while she noodled with her salad and drank a glass of tea. Bet she held down that booth an hour or two at a time. Tough on me when we had a big crowd and I didn't have that booth free to get fresh tips. Jackie always left a small tip, even though she held that space long as she did. If she left me over a dollar, I think she might have cried herself to sleep about it. Cheap as she could be. Ah, maybe I'm catty 'cause all the men liked her. I remember when I used to be something on a stick, and now I've just got the stick, so being honest, you got to measure that against what I say about her. That's all I got, Hap."

She eased away. Leonard said, "No one has thrown us out for being a black-and-white pair yet."

"Don't think they will. Don't think Professor has that kind of power. He wants it to be subtler, under the table. Where the Klan burned crosses and wore hoods, he wants to seem like a businessman. He'll take your money no matter what color you are, but try and buy a home in this town, set up a business, and your skin is black, he wants to keep that from happening. That's what he's working on. Separate but equal, he calls it."

Sharon brought the check and left. I was about to give the

check to Leonard, remind him it was his turn, when I noticed there was a folded note with it.

I palmed it flat on the table and read it.

Come by at midnight and I can tell you something about Jackie. Can't now. The wrong ears might hear. Like the redhead in the booth near the kitchen. I really do wish you'd asked me out a second time. Come alone, please.

There was an address below that.

I slipped Leonard the note and glanced toward the booth Sharon had indicated.

The redheaded fellow seemed to be woolgathering as he sipped his coffee. Me and Leonard might as well have been on Mars, the way he acted. Had he been following us? Maybe Jimmy and Lou had traded off because we knew their truck, would recognize them. Could it be like that?

"We could just go over and ask Red there if he'd like his meal jammed up his ass, get this over with," Leonard said.

"We could, but to me that seems like a bad approach to investigation, as well as a waste of mediocre food."

"Might be," Leonard said. "I can tell you clearly, though, you aren't going over there by yourself tonight."

"Hey, never intended to."

19

We had nothing else to do for a while, so I drove us out across the Sabine River Bridge again.

"I think we should get a hotel in Tyler for tonight, come back when it's dark," I said.

"Yeah, all right. I got an idea or two I want to chase. But before I work those ideas, I want to canoodle with them, think them over."

"That is so sweet," I said. "Canoodling with your ideas."

We ended up in Tyler at a Holiday Inn. We hauled our overnight bags up to the third floor, made coffee in the room, sipped and sat on our beds opposite one another, and talked.

"I told you I had some ideas," Leonard said.

"You were canoodling with them," I said.

"Yes, and after much hugging and kissing them, I kind of came up with a thing or two, and then that thing or two gave me another idea or two."

"All that canoodling has caused your ideas to multiply," I said.

"Other night, we're in the house where Jackie used to live, and

Ace shows up. I'm thinking he must have known she was long gone from there, and why would he think our car was Jackie's car? He would know her car."

"Could have thought she got a different car," I said.

"Considered that. What are the odds Ace drives by where Jackrabbit used to live, decides our car might be her car, a car he doesn't know? Maybe he came there looking for something, and then he saw us and thought we were looking for the same something."

"Something hid in the house?" I said.

"It's a long shot, but I been thinking that way."

"Couldn't Ace easily have come back since we last saw him, got whatever was there? Provided something was there."

"Could have, no doubt," Leonard said, "but maybe after he found us there, got his ass handed to him, he decided to stay away."

"Actually, if you count him hitting me with a chair, he came out all right."

"I was talking about me. I whipped his ass while you were stretched out on the floor. But if I'm right, and he wants what's there, he can't be cautious for long. Place might get rented out, and if there's something hidden there, it'll be harder for him to get to it then."

"Didn't look to be a place riddled with secret hiding places," I said.

"No," Leonard said, "it didn't, but I'm thinking something could be there just the same. Good chance he did go back and get it, but I think we ought to take a peek."

"Sounds reasonable," I said.

"I got another idea too, but for that one I'm going to need some gloves and a pair of bolt cutters, and if I get the chance, I'm going to order me one of those hats like Ace has."

20

After we left the hotel and shopped for some gloves and a nice pair of bolt cutters for Leonard, we came back there and holed up for a few hours, waiting for dark. I read the book by Rocky Hawkins about growing up in Gladewater, Texas. He knew his business. I had grown up in nearby Marvel Creek, and Gladewater seemed almost exactly the same. His father had been a gangster, one of the East Texas kind, and he knew a lot of the same people I had met in passing or knew of through story and perhaps legend. It was a short book and Rocky liked religion a lot better than I did, but he wrote simply and with heart. I came away from the book liking him and finding the book fascinating and honest as a dead hog.

Leonard read too, and about an hour before the sun sank, we put on the darkest clothes we had, fixed another cup of coffee to fortify ourselves, loaded up the gloves and bolt cutters, and away we went.

By the time we arrived back in Marvel Creek, it was solid dark and a light rain had started and the lights of the town gave the wet streets an eerie quality.

We drove as many back streets as possible, since with the town not being all that big, we didn't want to chance an encounter with Jimmy and Lou or for that matter the redheaded guy, who we figured also worked for the Professor. There was even a chance Professor or George might be in town for a big fandango at the Mexican restaurant, a fandango that would have consisted of some tinny Mexican music and some good food.

There was, of course, the twins to think about. They had said not a word and done nothing but walk and stop and stand, and from experience, I knew they were the ones to truly fear.

We parked at the side of the street where the movie-theater-now-church was, put on the gloves we had bought, and took a short walk over to the house, trying not to look as conspicuous as we were. What worked in our favor was most of the town had already rolled up their sidewalks and were at home having dinner, visiting with family.

The thought of that made me wish I was home doing the same. I missed Brett. We may have been together for years, but we had only been married a couple days, and though nothing was actually any different than before, I felt we should be basking in our recent decision together.

The rain was a mist now and the air was cool. The house was dark and it still looked empty. We went along the walk as if we owned the place and could shit anywhere. At the back of the house we found it still locked, way we had left it. I held a penlight while Leonard worked the lock and got us inside.

We didn't try to turn on lights, of course. There may not have been any electricity anyway, but if there was, we didn't want to try it. The house had a very bad smell, and we knew that smell, and as soon as we closed the back door, Leonard said, "Aw, hell."

"Yep," I said.

We followed the smell trail, which grew stronger as we came to the bedroom we hadn't gone into last time. There was nothing of Jackie there in view. No pieces of paper with a new address on it. No cryptic messages written in chicken blood on the wall or whatever it is the detectives find in cozy mystery novels.

The bedroom with the stink looked a lot like the bedroom that didn't stink. There was no furniture. We could see dust circulating in front of the windows without curtains, spinning in the bit of golden glow that came from the backyard light of the house with the fence.

And we could see a body splayed out on the floor.

21

The body was on its back. The mouth and eyes were open, as if the corpse were trying to mime excitement. One hand rested on his thigh, the other arm was thrown wide; one leg had a knee lifted, the other was stretched out with its boot turned to the side. There was blood coming out from under the body. It had made a pool around the man's head, had dried dark and thick, as if he had lain down in a mass of spilled molasses.

As we neared the body, flies that had found their way in through some crack or another rose up from the corpse with a buzz, out of the body's mouth and off of its eyes. They were thick enough that the next-door neighbor's light shining through the window made them momentarily appear like a little black cloud or a misshapen and alien creature. They buzzed up and into one corner of the room and blended with the shadows there.

Nearby, covered in blood, lay Ace's silly hat, Leonard's most recent craving.

"Gonna take a flier here," Leonard said, "and guess this mother-fucker is dead."

We held our noses and I used my free hand to shine the light on him. It was Ace, of course. He had been dead for a while, proba-bly had come back to the house shortly after we left it.

There was more blood near the closet, and it had flowed under the door, and there was a footprint in the blood. It had dried. It was average in size.

I could see a partial footprint, the heel, visible just outside the closed closet door. I gave Leonard my flash, and he held the light on the footprints while I used my cell to snap some photos, though I feared they wouldn't come out as well as I wanted, the light being weak. I was hoping we might match the print to some-one's boots.

Being careful not to step in the blood, I opened the closet and Leonard shone the light around for me while I took a look. There was nothing there but more bloody prints.

There wasn't an attic entrance in the closet ceiling. No one had climbed inside the attic through the closet. There was a bit of masking tape dangling from the edge of the door frame in-side the closet. The masking tape was painted over the same color as the inside of the closet. I mentioned that to Leonard. It didn't mean anything to him either.

I made an effort to search Ace's body without stepping in blood. The odor he put off was terrible. Damn dead folks. I went through his pockets with my nose scrunched up.

"Goddamn hat's ruined," Leonard said.

"Yeah. That's a shame."

Ace had a wallet with five dollars in it, a package of rubbers, and a picture of three black kids, all boys, with a goat. I figured it was from his childhood. One of the kids looked like the guy Ace would grow up to be, though he appeared a lot happier in the photo than he did now. In fact, everyone in that photo, including the goat, looked pretty content.

The blood on the floor had all come from Ace's head. Someone had parted his hair with a hatchet. His skull was split down the center to the bridge of his nose, and some of his brain had oozed out like puke. That had been some lick.

In his pockets, I found some lint and thirty-five cents. I put the wallet and the thirty-five cents back, let the lint fend for itself.

I stood up and stepped off a way. That helped a little with the odor. Another minute close to the body and I would have thrown up. I could see from the next-door neighbor's light that the flies had moved from the corner of the ceiling and had gathered on the windowpane like some kind of decoration.

"Whatever he was looking for," I said, "he didn't seem to find it, or if he did, whoever whacked him took it, or maybe afterwards they looked around and found it. Or there was nothing here to begin with."

"Ace thought there was, and whoever whacked him upside the noggin thought so too," Leonard said. "Guess they could have come in with him, pretended to be a friend, and took him out. My guess, though, someone sneaked up on him. I mean, hell, someone carrying a fucking ax or hatchet would make a man suspicious, not to mention nervous. You'd pretty quick guess he wasn't your friend."

"See the way the sleeves of his shirt are bunched up at the elbows, pulled up on the wrist," I said. "He may have fought with them, stretching his shirt, or someone grabbed his arms from behind and someone else gave him the death stroke."

"That is so cute. A detective-type deduction."

"I thought it was pretty good," I said. "I mean, wearing long sleeves this time of year doesn't seem smart, but I won't get the chance to discuss that with him now."

"He was stylish-minded," Leonard said.

"You know, this happens to us a lot. Dead bodies, I mean."

"Yep. Just lucky, I guess. Long as we're here, let's look the place over. Maybe we'll find a serious clue."

"That would be too handy," I said.

"Well, now and then a fart don't stink too bad," Leonard said.

"What? That doesn't make any sense."

"It's over your head, Hap. Let it go."

Leonard had been flashing the light around the bedroom, and now he had the light pooled in a corner. There was something small and dark in the center of the bright pool, up against the wall.

I went over and picked it up.

"So, their hiding place was they put this in a corner of the house?" I said.

I was holding it up now and Leonard had the light on it. It was a thumb drive designed to look like a little man in a tuxedo, but his head was missing.

"I don't think so," Leonard said.

He flashed the light around some more, went over to a spot along the wall and picked something else up. He came back and gave it to me. I saw that it was the top of the thumb drive, a man's head wearing a top hat.

"What I think," Leonard said, "is Ace did find it, but the guys who killed him didn't know that. It was taped inside the closet wall with some masking tape, which explains that. But before he found it, it would have blended in pretty good. Whoever gave him the chop came in on him right after he found the drive. They surprised him, and when they hit him—"

"He reflexively tossed his hand out and away went the drive, only they didn't see that."

"Another thought is they might have been following Ace, wanted to take him out for some reason we don't know, didn't know there was anything to look for. Followed him to the house, killed him, and left. More I think about it, more I like that idea. They didn't know what he was looking for, didn't know he had found it, and didn't care. It was him they wanted, and they got him."

22

The rain had picked up and the streets were running with water. The rain was silver in the thin light from houses and it was cold as a wet eel as it slipped down my collar.

We walked carefully and quickly to our car, took off our gloves, sat in the car, and gathered our wits, which is a pretty short process most of the time. I turned on the heater for a few moments to cut the chill, and then it was too hot. I turned it off. We continued to sit there.

"I can still smell him," Leonard said. "I'd rather stick my head face-first into a bucket of horse shit than smell another dead body."

I agreed. I knew from experience that even when we were well away from the body, that stench would live inside of our nostrils for a time, and then after that, the memory of the smell would come back to us now and again as if we were still standing in that bedroom, looking down on his body.

We drove around looking for an old-style phone booth to drop a word to the police about the body, but we didn't find one. In this town, phone booths had gone the way of the magazine stand.

We knew better than to call from our cells, so we finally decided to let the whole thing go for the time being. It wasn't like Ace was going to have a resurrection if found.

Leonard said, "I don't want to be insensitive, but fuck Ace. He hit you with a chair."

"That chair did hurt."

"I want to let him lay for now, and you know where I want to go."

"Yeah," I said. "I certainly do. But there's no Dairy Queen here."

"I don't want ice cream, Hap. Remember the bolt cutters?"

"Oh yeah."

I cruised us on out to George's junkyard, and before long we were gliding over the top of the hill, looking down on the yard, which was spotted with booger lights and the rain gave the cars and the flattened stacks of them a kind of shimmer.

We were bold about it. Drove right up to the double gate. Leonard got out with the bolt cutters, snipped the chain that held the gates together, and pushed one of the gates open.

I drove inside and parked the car and stayed inside of it, watched as Leonard walked ahead. That's when I heard Rex. He was loose in the yard, as George said he would be, barking and growling, raising a ruckus. I could hear him running too, sounded like a herd of elephants stampeding between the cars. There was a stronger light near the gate, and it spilled wide over the ground, and soon Rex appeared in that light. He was demonic-looking, and I could almost imagine him with two more heads, Cerberus, serving as the guardian to the gates of Hell. He was charging right at Leonard.

Leonard bent down on one knee and dropped the cutters and held out both hands, palms down. I reached over and got the pistol out of the glove box and cracked the driver's door but didn't get out. I didn't want to get bit. I had already experienced rabid-squirrel trouble, and I didn't want to add a savage dog bite to my experiences.

Leonard said, "Rex, good boy," and I swear to you, that powerful dog quit barking and growling and slowed and came with his tongue hanging out of his wide mouth and ran right into Leonard's arms. I had never seen anything like it, and with Leonard I've seen a lot. He was like the dog whisperer right then. He cooed and talked to the dog and the dog licked his face and swabbed his ears with a tongue that seemed long enough and thick enough to use for a beach towel.

Leonard stood up slowly, bent and patted the dog, went over and opened the back door. Rex jumped in without hesitation. It was like he was making an escape from prison and we were his accomplices.

Rex leaned over the seat and licked me from the back of my neck to the top of my head.

"Yuck," I said.

Leonard was climbing in on the passenger side with the bolt cutters.

"That was impressive," I said.

"Learned it from our old friend Veil."

"I thought you guys hated each other."

"Only when we see each other. I talk to him on the phone now and again."

"Really? You guys talk?"

"Yep, that works best. No actual face-to-face contact. He

knows dogs. He knows I love them, and I think that's where we bond. He told me how to make a dog feel safe. A happy dog would have bit me."

"Thought it was more unlikely a happy dog would bite."

"A happy dog cares about his master, but an unhappy dog can be swayed."

"I'm not sure I would have trusted that idea," I said.

"It may be mostly bullshit when you get right down to it, but he didn't bite me."

"Yeah, you got that going for you."

"Asshole like George, he don't need to own a dog. Needs to own a coffin with himself in it, his black heart cut out and burned to ashes and poured in a ditch."

"That's your justification for dog theft?"

"It's not theft," Leonard said. "It's liberation. Let's go."

23

It was still early and there was really no place to go and for the moment nothing to do in Marvel Creek, so I drove us back across the Sabine River Bridge, wheeled us to Tyler and our hotel.

We walked Rex inside with Leonard using his belt like a leash, and Rex came along like he was the hotel manager. The kid behind the desk didn't say a word. I figured he didn't want to argue with two rough-looking customers and a pit bull that was possibly the manager.

We sat in our room for a while and didn't talk much, which wasn't like us. I always hear how men don't talk, and maybe that's true of some, but you normally couldn't shut me and Leonard up, and right then we had nothing to say, and if we did, no way to say it. The shared experience of finding Ace was enough to hold us for a bit.

Rex climbed up on the bed with Leonard and lay his head in Leonard's lap. I had some jerky sticks in my bag. I got up and gave a couple of those to Rex. He ate them with about two smacks apiece. When he was finished eating, he looked at me hopefully. I spread my fingers to show him I was all out. He understood and lay his head back in Leonard's lap. I sat on my bed and watched Leonard stroke Rex's scarred head. The dog closed its eyes and pretty soon I could hear him snoring.

I don't know when I came undone from it all, but I finally got up, fixed us more coffee, and got Rex another jerky stick. He was awake by then. I think he heard me rustling in the package that held the jerky. Sleep came second to eating for dogs.

We had our coffee and Rex had his stick, and then we sat around for a while longer and finally started talking.

"What are we going to do with the thumb drive?" Leonard said.

"Stick it in a computer, of course," I said.

"I'm thinking something hidden like that might not be easy to crack, unless we know the code. We can try just poking it in the computer, but I don't think it's going to be that easy. If it isn't, you know who we need?"

I did. Mercury. He was a computer wizard, among other things. He used to work at the Camp Rapture newspaper, but recently they decided they didn't need him to do what they'd had him doing, which was transferring all the old records and newspaper articles, which went back about fifty years, to modern computer storage. News and facts had lost prominence to glossy ads and bullshit.

They gave Mercury a party and a plaque and two weeks' severance pay, and sent him home. He had worked there for a large part of his life, but in the end, it was only a little different than him having wandered in off the streets. That's company dedication for you.

Mercury worked out of his home now, mostly computer repair and a bit of consulting, but he was still the best there was when it came to deciphering difficult data, and if Leonard was right, we might have some for him to decipher.

It could turn out to be nothing, might contain photos of Jackie in Disney World wearing a Minnie Mouse hat. Maybe just the hat.

We put the thumb drive in Leonard's overnight bag. Leonard put the belt on Rex again, took him outside for a walk while I waited upstairs. About fifteen minutes later Leonard and Rex came back.

"Manager said something about Rex this time," Leonard said. "He's not welcome."

"Well, shit."

"Let's take our bags and go. We've been thrown out of better places than this."

"And frequently."

The three of us left the hotel. The rain had stopped and the air tasted good and it had a slight chill. As Tyler was much bigger than Marvel Creek, we were able to find an all-night place for coffee fairly easy.

The café had some tables outside, and we could have Rex with us out there. He was still on Leonard's belt leash. Rex lay at our feet under the café awning and quivered from time to time in his sleep, made noises that almost sounded like a chuckle. I think he was delighting in his assisted escape from the junkyard, dreaming of better days eating jerky and humping lady dogs.

"I got this feeling maybe there's something about all this that isn't what we think it is," I said. "Like looking in a fun-house mirror and seeing a distorted image. That's what I think we're looking at. The distortion."

"Fair enough," Leonard said. "Always is a little of that, I suppose. Distortion, I mean."

"Might be more of it this time than usual," I said.

That was it for profundity. We sipped coffee. It was the last cup I intended to have for a while. One more and I'd be dancing down the highway juggling my nuts.

There was a surviving phone booth next to the café, and I used it to drop a call to the Marvel Creek Police Department. It had been so long, I had almost forgotten how the damn thing worked. Turned out Eula was not only the receptionist, she was also what served as a dispatcher in a small town like Marvel Creek. Add to that part-time mistress to Delf, and I wondered when she slept. Maybe while she and Delf were having sex.

I tried to disguise my voice by putting my hand over my mouth and talking between my fingers. I don't know if that did anything at all. I told her there was a dead body in an empty house and gave the address. I told her there was a funny hat there as well, and it wasn't salvageable. She didn't seem to recognize my voice and made no comment about the hat.

I bought Rex a hamburger, hold the lettuce and tomato, and he woke up long enough to eat it. We all got in the car and started slowly making our way back to Marvel Creek, Rex sitting behind us, licking the backs of our heads. When we were about halfway to Marvel Creek, Rex lay down, rolled onto his back, and, with his paws in the air, went to sleep.

"Poor baby," Leonard said, looking over the seat. "Eating that hamburger tired him out."

"I think it was licking our heads that wore him out," I said. "I feel like I need a hair dryer."

"Or, better yet, more hair," Leonard said.

"Says the man who has started cutting his short."

"It's the style, Hap. If there is one thing I am, it's stylish."

"Yeah. That's it."

When we crossed the Sabine River Bridge we were the only car out there. A high mist was rising off the water and it was entangling itself in the trees on both sides of the riverbank and blowing across the road in slow motion.

I pulled over and put the address my former schoolmate Sharon had given me into the GPS, then continued onward.

It was eleven thirty.

24

The house wasn't in town but on the outskirts near what we used to call the Gilmer Highway. It sat off the highway a goodly distance but could be seen from there. There were houses behind Sharon's house, and they went back a way and were separated only by small yards.

There were a few well-cared-for trees in the yard, and there were lights on behind the windows of one large room. A car was parked under a carport.

"She said come alone," I said, "so that's what I want her to think I've done."

"That's all right," Leonard said. "I'll sit with Rex and the gun. Something looks or sounds fishy, I'll be there like a shot."

I cruised past her house, turned around, and parked in her driveway. Leonard slid down in the seat and waited there with the gun from the glove box in his hand.

As I made my way up the walk, I saw through the trees that there was a white pickup parked out to the side of her house, behind some hedges. It wasn't exactly hidden, and it might not mean anything. Maybe the truck had got up in the middle of the night and drove itself there, perhaps liking the view. Maybe the truck belonged to the owners of the house behind Sharon's house.

But in for a penny, in for a pound, the motto of the dedicated investigator, the mantra of a fool.

I knocked gently on the door. Hardly any time went by before Sharon opened it. She was still wearing her waitress outfit. She smiled at me. It was another of those moments when she was a girl again, back in high school, with a line of suitors.

"Come in," she said.

I did. I stood near the door and waited. "You have something more to tell me?"

"I do. Something to show you. Wait one minute."

She went down a hall and turned into a room and out of sight. I rocked on my heels. It was a nice house. Too many knickknacks for me, but nice. I could see into the kitchen from where I stood. There was a large clock on the wall with a white background. It was an old-style clock, not digital. The black hands really stood out. I watched the second hand swing around in a circle a few times.

Perhaps Sharon didn't have any information, and she was changing into a negligee, hoping to rekindle that old school spirit. That would be awkward. Brett didn't let me date.

After a moment I heard movement, looked up. Sharon was coming out of the room at the back and she wasn't wearing a negligee. The redheaded man from the café was with her. He wasn't wearing a negligee either. He had a gun held down against his leg. I would have preferred the negligee.

Sharon looked wimpy. She stepped to the side so that the redhead was directly in line with me. He patted his thigh with the gun. He smiled the kind of smile a shark does right before biting the head off a tuna.

I said, "I wasn't expecting a threesome. But before we start, I don't do anal. Or anything that involves rubber dicks and lube oil."

Redhead kept smiling. It wasn't because he liked my humor. "You try and run, I'll pop you. I can shoot quick as a cat can jump."

"But can you hit anything?" I said.

"That too. Don't believe me, try me."

"Sorry, Hap," Sharon said. "Professor, he says for you to do something in this town, you do it, even if you don't agree with it. For the record, I don't, but he said, so I did."

"That's all there is to it?" I said. "You're a Judas because Professor says you ought to be?"

"Red here made me an offer. I need the money. And he said he'd break one of my arms if I didn't."

"I let her choose which one," Red said.

"Well, damn, that sure makes me feel a sight better," I said.

"I am sorry. Really, Hap. I meant what I said today. I wished you'd asked me out a second time."

"You're just making it sweeter," I said. "So, they really call you Red?" I said.

"Sometimes. Where's the nigger?"

"She said to come alone."

"But where is he?"

"A hotel in Tyler," I said.

"Which one?"

I told him where we had been but didn't mention we had checked out. I told it convincingly, I thought.

"Bet you figured you were going to get you some nooky, didn't you?" Red said. "Sorry you're going to miss out. She's got some good stuff. This is done, I might be coming back to see her."

Red reached out and patted Sharon's ass with the gun.

Sharon turned bright red. I thought that was swell. That was sweet. She turned red because she got her ass patted, but she was fine with giving me to the wolves. It doesn't take all that much to go to the cops. She could have done that.

"I've dipped my wick there a few times, haven't I, honey?" Red said.

Sharon didn't answer, just looked straight ahead, sad and still blushing.

"What I'm going to want you to do," Red said, "is go out the door there and then out to your car. You're going to drive me and you where I tell you to drive. Later, I'm going to get the nigger. Divide and conquer. Always the best way to do it. Coming alone, that was stupid, boy."

"So, Professor has all this power, but he just sends you?" I said.

"One town, one ranger," he said.

"You're no Texas Ranger," I said.

"Easy-peasy. You get popped, then I'll have to give the nigger some attention."

"Might not like the attention you get back," I said. "You're going to need you, the twins, and maybe a pet alligator."

"Sure," Red said. "Go. Out the door."

I went out. Red prodded me with the pistol in my back, pushed me toward my car. I couldn't see Leonard in it.

When we got to the driver's side, Red said, "You drive where I tell you to drive, and you live longer. I might have you drive out somewhere far away and let you out and take your car. George pays for cars to be mashed up by that fucking machine. He gets through, don't matter who owned it. What's left you could slip under a door. Course, way it might work is I could leave you in the car when he mashes it. I could do that. I'll let you worry about which I'm going to do. And drive carefully and slow. I get carsick when I'm not driving."

"Like I give a shit," I said.

He popped me one in the back of the head with the barrel of the pistol. It wasn't too hard, but it wasn't a love tap either.

I opened the car door, looked for Leonard. He wasn't in the car.

Red said, "Wait a minute. I want to check."

He pushed me aside, had me stand back about four feet. He leaned inside the car, over the front seat, and took a look at the backseat, and that's when Rex hit him. I had forgotten about him.

It was like a shark attack. Rex's wide jaws clamped on Red's face, right over his nose and mouth. The impact of it was like a punch, knocking Red back and onto the ground, the dog coming out after him, close as a natural appendage, his body a mass of coiled muscle.

I stepped on Red's gun hand while Rex tore a large chunk of Red's face off and then grabbed him by the throat and bit deep, making a sound like someone snapping a crisp celery stick. Blood gurgled like coffee in a pot.

Red's hand went limp. He let go of the gun. I kicked it under the car.

Leonard came out from the bushes holding the automatic. He stood where he was, across the way from me, watching Rex work.

Sharon came to the door, put a hand to her mouth, and let out some air. Red was being whipped around by Rex as if he were wet laundry. I felt drops of blood land on my face. Red tried to scream, only managed to make a sound like someone gargling peanuts, and then he didn't make any more noise besides what his swinging body made on the gravel in the driveway. After a moment, I could hear bones cracking in Red's face.

I had no idea a dog could be that strong. Red had to weigh two hundred pounds, but he might as well have been a feather the way Rex manhandled him.

"Bad dog bite," Leonard said.

"I'll say."

Leonard walked over to me. "Shall we call Rex off?"

Rex had quit shaking Red, was just holding him to the ground by the neck with his jaws.

"Don't think it matters much now."

I looked to Sharon. She stood in the doorway. She was gray as ash in the porch light. She had one hand against her throat, as if to protect it from a dog attack.

I said, "Rex doesn't like people pushing his friends around."

"Oh Jesus," she said.

"You should have asked for him a little earlier," I said. "I think he shows up now, it'll be too late. Jesus couldn't resurrect that motherfucker. Only way he gets up is with a forklift."

25

The interrogation room was much nicer than the one in LaBorde or, for that matter, any I had ever been in, and I have experience.

It was small, but it was very neat, and you could smell the freshness of the wood paneling. There was a nice long table with no scratches on it, and Leonard and I were sitting on one side of it with our hands on the table. Our hands were free now, but we had worn handcuffs earlier, when Delf had us picked up by a very nice big black policeman with a very big gun.

That was all right. I was the one that called the cops to come out.

Delf came in. He wasn't as friendly this time. He looked at us like a housewife spying rot in store cabbage. He sat down. He had a notepad in his hand. He placed that carefully on the table. He glared at us the way Marvin looks at us. It made me feel homey.

"This is a nice room," Leonard said.

Delf ignored him.

"Sharon, she backs up your story. Said she had no choice but to set you up. She was under threat of death."

"I believe that," I said, "but that doesn't mean I like it."

"How's Rex?" Leonard asked.

"Animal control," Delf said. "They're considering putting him down."

"Don't do that," Leonard said. "He was in our car, minding his own business, when Red tried to look inside. Red had a gun, I might add."

"You had a gun too," Delf said. "And it's not registered to you."

"It's Hap's. I could see a man with a gun through Sharon's windows. I got the gun and got out of the car. Also, I had to pee. Rex hadn't got him, I would have. Rex isn't at fault here. He's my dog and he was protecting the car we were in while I was pissing in the shrubs."

"What's funny," Delf said, "is that dog looks exactly like the dog Junkyard George owns, and here's another coincidence. That dog's name is Rex too."

"Do tell," Leonard said. "Pretty popular dog name, huh?"

Delf took a deep breath and let out a tubercular-sounding sigh.

"Red set me up," I said. "He planned to get rid of me, and Leonard was next. He wanted us divided to make it easy. Sharon said to come alone. I didn't. I had Leonard and Rex."

"Yeah, well, as I said, Sharon tells pretty much the same story," Delf said. "Let me tell you something. I believe you guys. I believe her, for the most part. I could make a big deal out of this, but we're going to call it self-defense by use of dog. I'm not going to put in my report you stole the dog."

"That's very nice of you," Leonard said.

"Is, isn't it?" Delf said. "I don't like Professor, don't like what he had in mind for you. Don't care much for Sharon either. Red wasn't with her the whole time. She said he came over about ten, waited. She knew he was coming. She could have called and told me. I could have set him up. She likes the money they were going to pay her more than she liked you not being killed. I believe she was threatened, but she had a way out and she didn't take it."

"My sentiments exactly," Leonard said. "And that cheeseburger, at the place where she works. They use funky cheese."

"You know," Delf said, "they do. Kind of, I don't know, chewy, and not in a good way."

"Exactly," Leonard said. "What about Rex? Can I have him back?"

"I don't think George needs him. I'll have him brought over to you. They got him all muzzled and shit. Pit bulls, they can be dangerous."

"Only if you make them that way," I said. "Rex, he did what he did because Red pushed me. He likes me. He didn't care for Red. He loves Leonard. He ought not to be blamed for defending me and the car. He hadn't, me and my car might be flat and in a pile out at George's junkyard."

"Did Red say George wanted it done?" Delf asked. "Getting rid of you two, though, I'm beginning to understand why someone would want to."

"He said Professor wanted us taken care of, and he talked about having George crush my car with me in it," I said.

"That's thin," Delf said. "You say it, but Red can't say now that he said it. Professor and George can deny it. It's nothing, really."

"But Sharon backs it up," I said.

"She does, but some lawyer wants to play it cute, they could say she's covering her ass. Could say Professor wasn't in on this shit, just her and Red for some reason. They'll find a reason. Still, I'm talking to Professor and George. One of them might drop a ball and not mean to."

Delf sat there for a long while saying nothing.

We said nothing.

The air conditioner made a peculiar sound. It was kind of cold in there.

"Now, here's something else," Delf said, "and I just throw it out there, because I don't believe in this being just one of those things, since all manner of shit has been happening since you two came to town. But does the name Ace mean anything to you?"

We both shook our heads.

Delf studied us as if the word LIE was stamped on our foreheads.

"Big black guy, about the size of a tree, wore a bear-ear hat and used to date Jackie, the missing girl whose father turned up dead? I know you know some of this story. Jackie used to live with George until she got some kind of Martian mind-meld and got smarter and figured out George and her whole family and the whole fucked-up religion they belonged to was bogus . . . the name Ace still doesn't ring a bell?"

"Oh," Leonard said. "That brother. Yeah. We know who he is, but dead? Wow. That's some shit."

"Ain't it?" Delf said. "I didn't say he was dead, now, did I?"

"I'm a good guesser," Leonard said.

"Then you do know him?"

"Jackie's mother told us about him," I said, "and not happily."

"That whole nigger-in-the-woodpile business made her nervous," Leonard said.

"Did it now?" Delf said.

"And Jackrabbit's brother, Thomas," Leonard said, "he kind of gave us a vibe like he might think Jackrabbit ought to be killed for riding a brother's dick. Didn't you get that vibe, Hap?"

"I did."

"Someone took what was probably an ax to his head and left him in the house where Jackie used to live," Delf said. "I got to wonder why he was there, and who killed him, and who called in that he was murdered. Call turned out to be from a phone booth in Tyler, Texas. Where were you guys holed up?"

"Tyler," I said.

"Pretty coincidental," Delf said.

"Naw," Leonard said, "lots of people stay in Tyler."

"Uh-huh," Delf said, but he left that line of questioning alone. He turned to another. "Was Jimmy or Lou mentioned in any of this business by Red? You know, them being involved."

"Nope," I said.

"The twins?"

"Nope."

"Know what? I'll be glad when I can let you two go home. Or to prison. Or to a home for the demented. Someplace other than here."

"Lot of people feel that way," I said.

26

We spent the night in a jail cell. It's cheaper than a Holiday Inn. It was a small room with bars and the door was locked. We had one shitter and a bunk bed. I got the bottom bunk, Leonard got the top. Unlike Holiday Inn, the cell had room service of a sort. They fed us sandwiches. That's a plus.

Delf said us being in jail for the night was all for show.

It seemed real enough, though.

During the night, I dreamed of Rex and Red, how Rex's teeth ripped Red's face, how his jaws clamped on Red's head and crushed it like a Chinese paper lantern. The memory of it was so intense, I awoke several times. I glanced at Leonard's bunk. He was sound asleep.

Son of a bitch.

Come morning, about six thirty, we were let out of our cozy little room by the big black cop that had picked us up. He had his cap pushed back on his head. He was heavy around the middle and had legs like railroad ties. He had a face that looked to have collected some violence.

"Good morning," he said as we rolled out of bed, still wearing last night's clothes, of course. They didn't even spring for little orange pajamas.

"And good morning to you," Leonard said as he dropped down from the top bunk.

The cop unlocked the door.

"Y'all can come out," he said. "I'm supposed to take you so you can have breakfast. I'll eat with you. We didn't have an introduction last night, since I was putting you in cuffs, but my name is Johnny Williams. Breakfast will be your treat."

He drove us over to the café in a cruiser. I had yelled for shotgun, so Leonard got the backseat. It was no longer raining, but from the night before the streets were as shiny as a snotty nose.

"This was not a nice place for us yesterday," I said as we sat in the car in front of the café. "We ordered food and ended up getting snookered."

Johnny sat behind the wheel of the cruiser and grinned across the seat at me.

"Wasn't that bad a day," Johnny said. "Your dog ate a bad guy. Really, he ate a bad guy's head. And you got to sleep in a nice comfortable room, and you aren't being arrested or detained, and you're getting your dog back, and you're about to buy me a nice breakfast, so how bad could it be?"

"When you put it like that," I said, "not bad."

Johnny nodded at the café.

"Place is all right, it's the owner that sucks shit through a straw."

"Professor," I said.

"Yep. He's not the actual on-paper owner, but he's the owner.

Got money invested, got a deal made with the lady who owns it on paper. He could sink her anytime he wants, so she toes the line. Deal he has with her pretty much goes like a lot of deals he has in town. You get to do what you want until he don't want you to do it anymore."

"What we heard," I said.

"A hungry black man like myself comes through, they'll feed him at the café, but a black man won't work here, and he won't own businesses in town or buy property. No new ones, anyway. And Professor prefers you not be supportive of the black people already here, most of them living in what we can politely call a collective spot on the far side of town. Plan is, Professor is going to gradually lily-white this place. Which is why Delf hired black officers on the force, to not have the town completely in his sweaty palm."

"That's also how we heard it," Leonard said.

"People here, hell, most of them moved on from all that real hard-core racist shit years ago. Thing is, they got to live in this town, so they are sometimes what I like to refer to as overly cooperative with Professor. They like black people individually, it's when they start thinking of them as a group that things get shitty. They seem to think all black folks are on welfare except the ones they know and like. Or they're doping it up or committing crimes. Let's go inside. I want Professor to hear that two brothers were in here today along with one white asshole, and who knows, tomorrow there may be four, then eight brothers. I like to think that kind of stuff keeps Professor pissed."

"Good enough reason to eat here," Leonard said.

"By the way," Johnny said, "Sharon will not be serving today. She has a few things to answer for, and maybe for some time, and she'll be answering at the jail. We are not being as nice to her as we were to you. She's still in a cell and she will be having a very cheap breakfast. Has all the nutrients necessary, though. We are not savages."

"What about Professor and George?" I said.

"Chief is talking to them, plans to talk to his own brothers as well. Chief's all right. Full of shit a lot of the time, but aren't we all?"

"And the twins?" I said.

"Nothing to talk to them about right now," he said.

Johnny got out of the car, and we followed.

Inside, a couple folks gave us the look, but most went about their business, filling their bellies before they headed to work. Johnny smiled and nodded at a few of them. No one called him names or burned a cross.

We found a booth at the side, the one Sharon claimed Jackrabbit occupied when she came in and ordered tea and a salad and left small tips.

A very tired-looking older lady with dyed-black hair who walked like a pirate with a peg leg waited on us. She wasn't chatty, but she was efficient. She took our orders and went away.

"That lady right there," Johnny said, referring to our waitress. "She works two jobs to take care of her kids. Husband ran off with some floozy and actually got run over by a bus, him and the floozy both. He had signed his insurance over to the floozy, and it ended up somehow that the floozy's drunk-ass mother got it. Fifty thousand dollars to that piece of shit, an old hag that hadn't worked at anything more than fifteen minutes in her life, and that fifteen minutes she was most likely trying to con some poor retard out of a dollar. And his wife, the waitress here, she didn't even get his best wishes or a finger up the ass. Woman like that works hard to take care of her family. She's like most of this town. Basically good."

"Basically ain't always enough," Leonard said.

"I think this place can be as good as any," Johnny said.

"Ain't you the little optimist," Leonard said. "You and Hap should get together for a sing-along."

"I got hope," Johnny said. "But I'm not foolish. Professor doesn't get dug in too deep, there's a chance. He does, it's like a seed tick gets in your balls and you try to pull it out, and the head breaks off in you. That's hard to get rid of."

"Damn, now I'm really hungry," Leonard said.

Actually, he was, and so was I. We ate and were on another round of coffee when Delf came in. He came over and sat by Johnny. He looked like he had been up all night.

"You want something to eat, Chief," Johnny said, "they're buying."

"I'll just have coffee . . . wait. You two are buying?"

"Looks like it," I said.

"All right, then," Delf said and summoned the waitress, gave her his order. "I'll have coffee, steak and eggs, a side of toast."

"You talk to Professor?" I asked.

"Him and George. They got nothing, of course. Said they talked to you two, that you were looking for Jackie and they didn't have any information and that's all there was to it. George said his dog is missing."

"He ought to put out some flyers," Leonard said, "maybe run a missing-doggy ad in the paper."

"What I told him," Delf said. "Johnny here explain our position on you two sticking your noses into our business?"

"I haven't yet," Johnny said. "Not really. But here it is in a nutshell. Don't get caught. Otherwise, do what you have to do."

"And if we do get caught?" I asked.

"Sucks to be you," Delf said.

"It's like that, is it?" Leonard said.

"That makes me nervous," I said. "It has . . . how shall I say it? A scapegoat sound. What if we decide this job isn't for us and we just get our dog and leave town?"

"That's fine too, but if you decide to come back, and you will, remember the ground rules," Delf said.

"What makes you think we'll come back?" I said. "Folks who hired us, we've used their time and money up."

"I don't think the money matters all that much to you. You leave, you'll be back."

"How could you know?" I said.

"Because I remember how you were in high school, Hap. How you crossed the color line when it was obvious it would cause you grief. I didn't do that, and I'm ashamed I didn't. Saying you're not a racist is not the same thing as living like you aren't one. You leave, you'll come back. Neither of you strike me as easy to get rid of, and I think now this is about more than finding a missing girl."

"Don't give us too much credit," I said.

"Yeah, I start to think I'm being worked," Leonard said, "all this highfalutin talk makes my nuts shrivel up. It has a bit too much of King Arthur and the Round Table to it. Like you think you'll pull us in deeper than we are just so we can feel noble."

"Is it working?" Delf said.

"I'm not sure," I said.

"By the way, called Chief Hanson in LaBorde," Delf said. "Told him I knew you two, asked how you guys were back home, how you acted, asked about your character. He confirmed you both are assholes and hardheads but said he would trust you with his life but not to tell you."

"But you just did," I said.

"I can't keep a secret," Delf said.

27

We picked up Rex and drove back to LaBorde. Screw all that macho shit from Delf about how we'd be back. We got paid for two days and we did two days. It wasn't all that wonderful a couple days either, least not as far as our case went.

We arrived in LaBorde close to noon, parked in our office lot, opened up the car trunk where our luggage was. As Leonard prowled around in there, I saw the bicycle lady through the plate-glass window at the front of her business. She was still blond and pretty and she still liked to wear shorts. Really short shorts. She looked up and saw me and smiled.

I should add that I am noble of heart.

Leonard got the thumb drive out of his luggage and put it in his pocket. Rex stood with us, watching things carefully, as if he might be thinking about coming back to steal the car when we weren't looking.

The three of us climbed the stairs to the office, and when we came in, Brett was behind the desk with her laptop open.

"Porn?" I said.

"Of course," she said. "Well, almost. I been reading up on guys like Sebastian, people with his kind of inclinations. People who want to witness their own deaths. It's fucked up. You boys seem to have brought a friend."

"Yeah, he's just hanging," Leonard said.

There is a foldout couch in the office, and right then it was folded up and was just a couch. Leonard made a beeline for that, sat down. Rex jumped up on the couch beside him and put his head in Leonard's lap.

"Cute," Brett said. "Poor baby. He another rescue?"

"He is at that," Leonard said. "Last night he ate a bad guy, chewed his head up like a Tootsie Roll."

Brett stood up then and we embraced. I sat in a client chair and told her the entire story.

"Jesus," she said. "You boys have had a couple of bad days. And the police chief thinks you're coming back?"

"But we aren't," I said.

"Our lovely clients actually brought in some more money," Brett said. "I feel guilty taking it if you aren't going back."

"They're doing all right," I said. "Got a nice truck. They could do with paying a little extra. I got hit by a chair."

"I see the bruise on your noggin," Brett said.

"Will this allow me sympathy sex later?" I said.

"One never knows," she said. "Guys, I went to the address the Mulhaneys gave us and checked out where they lived. Patch of weeds outside of town with a trailer on it, and the trailer has one end burned off. Kitchen fire is my guess. They've put a tarp on that end to patch it, used lots of duct tape to hold it in place. The truck they have is better than that trailer."

"Duct tape is underrated even by those who love it," Leonard said. "Like a friend of mine, Eugene Frizzell, once said, you got duct tape, you can get to the moon. You know what, maybe the trailer burned up on one end because someone had one of those intense religious moments and burst into flames."

"I have no idea what that means," Brett said.

"It means don't underrate duct tape," Leonard said, scratching Rex's hard head.

"So, we got more money, and you can afford to go back, or we can return their dough," Brett said, "just claim the two days we got paid for. Tell them what you found out and call it a day. It's nothing definitive, but it's what you know."

"I don't like them," Leonard said. "They're not the first folks who've lived in bad trailers. I lived in a ragged one, right out of the military. I've lived in houses with walls so thin the wind stayed inside instead of out."

"What do you think, Hap?" Brett said.

"Well, we did find something," I said.

Leonard stretched out a bit on the couch so he could get his hand in his pocket and pull out the thumb drive. "We got this."

I leaned out of my chair, took it from him, and gave it to Brett.

"That's the one thing I hadn't told you about yet," I said, and then I told her how we had come by it.

"Damn, you boys have certainly cracked a few eggs," she said.

She put the thumb drive in the laptop, and we waited.

"Nope," she said. "Not happening. It's coded."

"Not surprised," I said. "It may be nothing but personal porn or a pie recipe, but it may also be something more important, and it's maybe what got Ace killed."

"Still don't think the people killed him were looking for that,"

Leonard said. "Think their beef was with Ace himself. Followed him there, gave him the ax."

We heard footsteps on the stairs. The door opened and Chance came in. She had her hair tied back and was wearing a loose shirt and jeans and slip-on tennis shoes. I thought she looked cute as the proverbial bug.

I got up and hugged her, and she went around behind the desk and hugged Brett.

"Don't forget old Uncle Leonard," Leonard said.

Chance went to the couch and hugged him. She gave the dog a pat.

"What's his story?" she said, nodding at the dog.

"He's a client," Leonard said. "He lost his cat."

"Ha-ha," Chance said.

Leonard told the whole thing over again about how the dog was rescued, and then he told her about the case, all we had discovered.

"Oh yeah. Brett told me about the case," Chance said. "I wish I could have been more involved, but I've been taking a couple of college courses, so I've only been working part part-time. And I've been taking care of Reba a lot."

"That really shouldn't be your job," I said.

"Then whose job would it be?" Chance said. "She doesn't have anyone. I've been making sure she goes to school. She's smart as a whip, so she should go. She worries me, though. She said there was a little honky there she was going to pop a good one. I suggested she not do that."

"Probably has it coming," Leonard said.

"Agreed, but in time we may be hearing from child protective services," Brett said. "Honky-popping could certainly get them called in."

"She needs someone," Chance said. "She's like a little sister to me. She cusses worse than Dad and Leonard, though."

By this time Chance had taken a seat in the other swivel client chair. She spun in a circle and came back around to face us.

"You go back, you going to push until something blows?" Chance said.

"If we were to go back," I said, "that's exactly what we'd do. It's really all we know. But we don't know we're going back."

"They'll go back," Brett said.

"I don't know," Leonard said. "We're getting a little long in the tooth for the tough stuff. Divorce cases, sneaking around taking photos of some wife or husband doing the two-bear mambo, that's starting to be more our style."

"Damn right," I said.

"They'll go back," Brett said.

28

That night, at home, getting ready for bed, Brett said, "So Jackie thought she could move between dimensions?"

"According to some," I said. "I don't know if she thought that or not. Sounds to me like she was speaking theoretically. Of course, maybe we can't find her because she really did move into another dimension. She could be dead. She could be in Australia training kangaroos to dance the jitterbug."

"They would be good at that," Brett said.

"Thing is, everyone we talked to thought she was a little on the odd side, so maybe something to it, about her thinking something like that, thinking she could do it. And maybe she's merely talking quantum physics to a bunch of knot heads who have a hard time believing in a calorie because they can't see it."

Brett was beside the bed, pulling a nightgown over her head. When she had it on, she slapped her ass. "I believe in calories, unfortunately."

"You wear them beautifully," I said.

We got in bed and covered up.

"Jamesway, he might have been able to at least carry on a conversation with her," I said. "He seems like a bright guy."

"What was your take on him besides being bright?"

"Seemed all right, maybe someone using the bullshit of religion for good. To be honest, I liked him quite a bit, but man, he makes terrible coffee."

I turned off the light.

"Shit," I said.

"What?"

"You know."

"I do?" Brett said.

"Yeah. You know. I decided to face it just now."

"You and Leonard are going back," she said.

"I know I am."

"Then you know he is too."

"Pretty much. Yeah."

"I wouldn't want you to go without him."

"He wouldn't want me to either," I said.

29

Next morning I got dressed and called Leonard. Officer Carroll, aka Curt, picked up the phone.

"Hap," he said.

"Leonard there?"

"I stole his phone. I'm in Puerto Rico."

"I know better than that. Leonard can't afford the roaming, and you can't afford the trip."

"Okay, he's in the shower, which is a polite way of saying he's taking a shit."

"Have him call me, but wait until he's good and finished. I don't want him doing a half ass-wipe to hurry up and answer the phone."

Officer Carroll chuckled.

About twenty minutes later Leonard called me back.

"That was one hell of a shit," I said.

"Championship. I had burritos last night. We're going back to Marvel Creek, aren't we?"

"We are."

"Good. I was going to call you and suggest just the same thing. I already got Rex boarded with some friends of Curt's. I knew this was coming even when I said I didn't know it was coming."

"Yeah. Me too."

"I don't like being ran out of a town, or ran out of most anywhere, for that matter, unless I'm ready to go. Hey. Curt is off for a couple of days. He's going with us."

"Him being LaBorde law, could that cause him problems?"

"I'm only going to let him get involved so far, but I think he could be a help. I think you're slowing down a little, so I want some backup."

"Fuck you."

"Pack a lunch. Three sandwiches and some chips. We'll stop and get drinks. And clear out your trunk. Me and Curt will be rooming together, and I want space back there for a crate of rubbers. Now that I think about it, you might want to throw out the spare tire."

30

I drove. Leonard sat beside me, and Officer Carroll sat in the back, leaning over the seat like a Labrador retriever. He had brought enough luggage for a month in Paris and, along with that, a bulletproof vest.

"You really need the vest?" I said.

"Never leave home without," he said. "That and clean underwear."

I liked Curt, but he was kind of a pest, so it was like driving on a cross-country vacation with a six-year-old. We had already stopped twice. Once for soft drinks, once for Officer Carroll to pee, and now he wanted to go again.

"Pookie, I told you to go before we left," Leonard said.

"I was excited," Curt said. "Are we on a tight schedule?"

"Guess not," Leonard said.

"Pookie?" I said.

"I call him that," Leonard said.

"I kind of like it," Pookie said. "My dad used to call me Poot. I never cared for that much."

"I can understand that," I said. "From now on, I'll call you Pookie too."

"All right," Pookie said.

"Shit," Leonard said, "I should have never let that out in public."

We stopped and Pookie took another pee, and then on down the road, he said, "I wouldn't mind getting some coffee."

"Damn," Leonard said. "That's why you always got to pee."

"If we could stop someplace where they also got pie," Pookie said, "I'd like that best. I like pie. You guys like pie?"

"I should have left his ass at home," Leonard said.

· · ·

Brett had found us a bed-and-breakfast on the outskirts of Marvel Creek in a little community that would soon be annexed by the town. It was the only real place to stay unless we wanted to drive on to Longview.

Brett said according to the Internet photos, it was quite charming and, better yet, pretty cheap. The money we got from the Mulhaneys was not a fortune, but it was a fortune for them, as it would have been for me just a few years back. It was hard to believe there had been such a turn of fate in my life. I still had a lot of bad stuff going on, but at least now I could afford to be miserable.

Reminded me of my dad. He was a troubleshooter mechanic at one time for a butane company. Had to be on the road a lot, and he was, by all accounts, good at his job. Over time, he asked for a raise. It was promised, but it never seemed to make it into his paycheck.

Next time he asked for a raise, they said again, "Sure, we'll do that," but they didn't. And when he received his paycheck and saw the raise had still not been added, he went to his stall and began packing his tools in his toolbox. The boss came by, said, "Bud, what are you doing?"

"Well," Daddy said, "if I'm going to starve to death, I might as well be rested."

Anytime I thought about being in need of more money, I remembered that story.

Brett had checked us in online, and when the lady who owned the place saw one of our group was black and that he and Pookie intended to share a bed, you could see the hair on the back of her neck stand up. The rest of it was in a gray knot on her head.

"You know, I'm not sure that room is ready," she said. She reminded me of a nervous wasp, the way she flittered behind the desk. I had an idea her reluctance had nothing to do with Professor, who probably didn't own things this far out.

Still, our credit card looked better to her than her bullshit church-lady morals, so after a bit of nervous fluttering, she decided the room was ready and checked us in. When we left, she would probably bring in one of those hazmat teams that clean up oil and chemical spills, have them give Leonard and Pookie's room a real going-over, maybe burn the mattress.

"Breakfast is from seven until nine," she said. "After that, you're on your own."

Leonard laughed at her without really meaning to.

31

After I got my stuff stored in the room, I called Brett and asked about the thumb drive. She was supposed to get it to Mercury so he could see what was on it.

"You know," Brett said, "turns out Jackie is damn smart. Even Mercury couldn't crack it right off the bat. I drove over to Camp Rapture this morning, gave it to him, and after about twenty minutes he said he was going to need time."

"Wow. That is some serious encryption."

"That's what he said. I think he was impressed. It takes a lot to impress him with computer stuff."

"I'll say. Well, we are all tucked in. Pretty soon we go back to shaking trees to see what falls out of them."

"Be careful something big and mean and ugly doesn't fall out of one and land on you."

"Of course. Which reminds me, have I told you the joke about the gorilla hunter?"

"I don't believe in hunting gorillas."

"Neither do I. It's a joke."

"I think you've told me that one."

"I don't think I have," I said.

"Think you have. Don't remember all the details, but pretty sure you have."

"You don't want to hear my joke, do you?"

"Got to go, hon," and she was off the phone.

I actually have some pretty good jokes. I don't know why no one wants to hear them.

32

The best way we figured to stir things was to make sure we were seen, and one place we wanted to be seen was at the Coffee Spoon again. Everyone came there. Someone was going to slip a word to Professor, and that was bound to bring out some of his help. Jimmy and Lou maybe, George perhaps, the twins, someone we had yet to meet who wanted to shoot us in the back of the head or beat us to death with sticks and stones. It was always a pleasure to make new friends.

First, we drove over to Marvel Creek and the cop shop to talk with Delf.

"So, you're an officer of the law?" Delf said after we introduced Pookie and took seats in the office.

"I am," Pookie said.

"He's like fucking McGruff the Crime Dog," Leonard said.

"I am," Pookie said, "except I don't sleep in a doggy bed."

"What happened to Rex?" Delf asked.

"He's having a spa day," Leonard said.

"Knew you'd be back," Delf said.

"You called it," I said.

"I can be of assistance, but only to a degree. There's a line I best not cross, but I can cross some lines. You find something, tell me. Don't get yourself between a rock and a hard place. Also, Johnny, he's part of this. The other officers, not as directly. I handle them, but Johnny, I can give you his cell and you can contact him if necessary. You can tell him anything you can tell me."

"Thing is," I said, "you got your agenda and we got ours. Finding Jackie."

"Jackie, if she's found, is dead, my man," Delf said. "But our agendas cross enough we can be of help to one another."

"Guess that's true," I said.

"Good," Delf said. "Try not to shoot anybody."

"No promises," Leonard said.

"My brothers," he said. "Don't let them hurt you, but try not to hurt them. If possible."

"Deal," I said, and out of there me and Leonard and Pookie went.

33

We decided we weren't ready to hang out at the café drinking coffee, and it occurred to me another visit with Jamesway might be in order, and that seemed to suit Leonard and Pookie.

This time we came through the front door, which was unlocked, went through the lobby, and found him in his office with his feet on the desk reading a rather ragged-looking leather-bound copy of the Bible.

"Hap, Leonard," he said. "Good to see you. Who's your friend?"

We introduced Officer Carroll by his real name. I immediately feared coffee would be offered.

It was. Leonard and I declined. Pookie, not knowing any better, accepted. We left him to his fate.

"We're just going over our path again," I said.

"Meaning you haven't found Jackie, and you want to know if I know something. And you want to know if I had anything to do with Ace's death."

"We didn't say that," I said.

"But you were thinking it."

"Maybe," I said.

"I told you what I knew about Ace, and that's it. Next time I heard about him was reading about him in the newspaper, that he was found dead in Jackie's old house. What can I tell you I haven't told you?"

"It's just procedure," Pookie said.

"Procedure?" Jamesway said.

"I'm a cop," Pookie said. "I use cool cop terms. Don't get me started. I got a nest of stuff I can rattle off."

Jamesway smiled. "Ah."

"I don't know if we have any other questions," I said, "not really. But I'd like to come back to something. Just to touch it again and move on. Jackie's good with numbers, had what some call odd ideas. Was she odd or just smarter than the average bear?"

"Maybe both," Jamesway said. "You don't find bears doing mathematics or theorizing on the universe."

"Don't talk like you know all the bears there are," Leonard said.

Jamesway laughed a little.

"Did she believe she could travel between dimensions, alternate worlds, or some such?" I said.

"She's a thinker. Maybe even a genius when it came to mathematics and physics, and she had to learn most of it on her own. We used to talk for hours about all manner of things. Did she actually think you could do it, travel between the dimensions? The answer is, theoretically, yes, but she didn't think she herself could."

"She wasn't saying what they thought she was saying?" Leonard said.

"Not at all," Jamesway said. "Truth is, I miss our conversations. She could make you think, and I was attracted to her. I told you that. But there was always something kind of dangerous about her. Not that she did anything I could put my finger on. It was just a feeling she gave me."

Jamesway went over, fixed Pookie his cup of coffee, and brought it back to the desk.

I watched as Pookie picked up the cup and tasted the coffee. I thought Jackie might not have passed into another dimension, but with a sip of that stuff, perhaps Pookie temporarily had. One of his eyes twitched.

"Jackie wanted to do something with that brain of hers other than what she was doing," Jamesway said. "I think she decided she'd had enough of this hole in the road."

"You don't think she could be dead?" Pookie asked.

"I hope not. I think she had bigger fish to fry. I think she merely went away to someplace better. Someday, I believe she will resurface. She may not even be hiding. I'd check out the colleges in Tyler."

Brett had actually done that while I was home. Nothing found, but I didn't mention it to Jamesway.

"Nothing else?" Leonard said.

Jamesway shook his head. "Sorry . . . wait a minute. The librarian. Marylou Cinner."

"Librarian?" I said.

"Friend of hers. Well, she used to be a librarian. But she and Jackie got to be friends there at the end, meaning the end as in when I saw Jackie last. I sort of forgot about it. She didn't mention Marylou much, but she did mention her, and she said they were friends. I think Marylou, who was a quiet sort, was someone she could talk to about the things she was interested in. Someone to talk to smarter than the rest of us. I think Marylou had about three degrees or something, but what she was cut out for was being a librarian. I can't say I really knew her, but that's what Jackie said about her."

"Do you know Cinner's address?" I asked.

"I know where she lived. The house is empty now. Up for sale. It was repossessed. Didn't respond to foreclosure letters, or so I was told. One of the ladies works at the bank goes to church here, and she told me. If you're quiet, and you know connected people in this town, eventually they talk out of school. One day Marylou Cinner was working at the library, next day she was gone. Didn't give notice, just up and left. People went to the house, and all the furniture was there, but she wasn't, and there was a note. Note said she had a sick aunt and had to go take care of her, I think in Ohio. Something like that. Said she was sorry to leave so suddenly, and she was letting the house go back, and that was it."

"That's interesting," Pookie said.

"Yeah. Oh, and she was Ace's cousin," Jamesway said.

"Also interesting," Pookie said.

"Does it mean anything?" Jamesway said.

"If it does, we don't know what it is," I said. "Not yet, anyway." We thanked Jamesway and left.

On the way to the car, Pookie said, "That coffee is the worst thing I've ever put in my mouth."

"I got something for your mouth that can sweeten it," Leonard said.

"I know that, baby," Pookie said, and pinched Leonard on the ass.

34

We drove around town hoping to stir someone up, but no one was stirred. We went to the café and had lunch, but no one threatened us. We drove back to the bed-and-breakfast, but no one followed us. I looked out the window from my room. Nothing happening out there, though a large black bird on the lawn looked a little suspicious.

Maybe we had pushed as much as we could. Maybe Professor and his minions had got smart and decided to leave us alone and let us fade away. Maybe Professor had nothing to do with Jackie's disappearance. Perhaps Ace had been killed by someone who had nothing to do with either Jackie or the Professor. And Marylou Cinner, did she have anything to do with this? No fucking idea.

I sat down and turned on the TV and watched a bit of the news, but the political situation was so much like a shitty reality show, I turned it off before I got sick.

Brett called.

"It's your wife," she said.

"I love hearing that," I said.

"Here's something else you'll love. Thumb drive cracked. I picked it up from Mercury. A large part of it is numbers."

"That fits. She was a self-trained mathematician."

"Yep, but it's accounting. Nothing to do with any kind of super-math, but it is fanciful math at times."

"Come again," I said.

"It's records she kept. Way Mercury figured it, Jackie was the bookkeeper for Professor, and she started carefully moving money out of his account, disguising it as this and that, not something you'd notice right off, subtle stuff, but it was getting moved."

"Where to?"

"You're going to love this. It doesn't seem like anything at first. All legit, but she had a clever way to siphon the money off and have it end up somewhere else, and you know whose bank account it's in, and right there in Marvel Creek?"

"Do I have to guess?"

"Yep."

"All right," I said. "Her own account."

"Nope."

"How about Jamesway?"

"Nope. Your junkyard man."

"George?"

"Yep."

"That's a surprise," I said. "I thought he was Professor's man."

"George seems to have been his own man. He had this girl-friend who was a math whiz, and either he got her to do it or they were both in on it. Appears they began to slip money away from the Professor. Did it in small bits here and there. Never anything noticeable. Disguised as an expense, but the thing was, the expense was maybe half of what was used to pay out, and then part of the expense got transferred to this or that, traveling through channels, and pretty soon it's in George's bank account."

"I'll be damned. Might George not have known?"

"It was in his account," Brett said. "Surely he looked at his bank statements from time to time. There were several different companies under his name, and there were three banks, one in Marvel Creek, one in Longview, and another in Tyler. But in the end, they all came back to George."

"Damn interesting."

"Yep. But that's not all. Mercury figured that later, all that business was reworked. Not so you'd notice it unless you understood money and how to launder it and make everything look clean and on the up-and-up until all of a sudden you got nothing in your account, because what you see isn't what you get. It's all been boosted to another account. The figures in the former account are what Mercury calls ghost figures; the remains of dead money. George's bank accounts got shifted to Ace's bank account. Again, at a glance, George had money, but when you really looked carefully at the transfer numbers, Ace had it. Maybe Ace had something to do with it all too."

"Ace would be lucky to know which end the shit came out of an elephant even if he was standing under its ass."

"However it got there, it got there. But I'm not finished. Later on, Mercury figured out from all the revising what Jackie was doing. She was moving money from Ace's account to one Marylou Cinner's account."

"The librarian."

"What's that?"

I said it again and told her the little bit Jamesway had told us, including the fact Cinner had moved off.

"Now, that is interesting," Brett said.

"Yeah. It is. Cinner hasn't been a player on the field, and all of a sudden, she is. I'm wondering, did she mastermind all of this?"

"I'll see if I can find her by the usual routes, on Facebook, that sort of thing, and if that comes up goose egg, I'll see if Mercury can help me. He's still looking into the material on the thumb drive. He says there's more, he's just not sure what it all means. Looks like Jackie's long game might have been being aided first by George, then Ace, and then it went to Marylou Cinner's account. She may have been using them all as channels to take the money out and keep it for herself. Up to you to figure out what it all means. I have given you the tools to do your work, so now you can do it."

"I gave you the tools to find the tools," I said.

"True, but I'm your boss, and shit rolls downhill in a large stinky ball. Catch."

35

I went over to Leonard and Pookie's room, told them what Brett told me.

"Bottom line," Leonard said, "it's like that movie where they say follow the money. We follow that, we find what happened to Jackie and her baby, if there is one. All this talk about segregation, shit, it's the money, you wait and see."

"Why not go talk with George?" Pookie said. "He works for Professor, and us knowing George was stealing money from Professor, even if he didn't end up with it, might not be something he would want revealed. Could give us some leverage and make him cooperative."

"I like it," Leonard said.

"Me too," I said.

36

We got directions to George's home from Brett, but when we drove out there, there was a burned-down house with a washing machine in the yard, blackened by fire. No one had lived in that spot for a long time. Somehow, George had gone off the grid, at least temporarily.

Plan B was since we were close to Longview, we would drive over there, and Pookie would rent a car and drive back out to the hill over the junkyard, find someplace to park, and see when George headed home. For all we knew, George had left the day before and was on vacation in the Bahamas. But as it stood, Pookie observing him and following him home and then giving us a call with directions was the best we could come up with. We wanted to talk to him somewhere other than the junkyard, somewhere away from Professor's influence, should he coincidentally be at the yard.

We figured this was a good plan because George hadn't met

Pookie, and he didn't know the rental, but he knew my car and he knew me and Leonard.

By the time we got to Longview and rented the car and stopped to have coffee and a snack, because Pookie insisted, it was near what we thought would be George's quitting time.

Me and Leonard drove to a place not far from the junkyard but out of sight and parked and waited to hear from Pookie. We hoped no one thought we looked suspicious.

We played I spy for a while, but there wasn't that much to spy, and Leonard cheated. He changed what he had spied if he thought I was figuring it out. It was like playing with a five-year-old, but with a nastier vocabulary.

After a bit, the rain, which had left us for a while, came back. The sky turned dark and the clouds rolled in and there were splashes of rain on the windshield.

Leonard's cell rang. "Got you," Leonard said into the phone, then clicked off. "Pookie is following him. We'll get a report from him with directions shortly."

Pookie called back, and we followed his directions. George didn't live far from the junkyard. He lived down a road that ran into a path through the woods. It was a narrow road of shipped-in caliche and it worked good for the tires in the rain.

We saw Pookie parked off to the side. He had the rental car turned around, facing us. We pulled up in front of him. He got out in the rain and ran toward us, slid into the backseat.

"Just a bit farther up the road," Pookie said. "Best to walk from here."

"Did he see you?" I asked.

"Please," Pookie said. "Fucking spy satellite couldn't have found me, I am that stealthy."

We got out in the rain and started walking. We didn't have umbrellas or raincoats. What we had was wet clothes and skin. It was a damn shabby night, and I felt pretty shabby myself.

Only good thing was we didn't have far to go.

George's house wasn't a house but a double-wide trailer that looked as if it had been recycled from a major storm event. The windows had cheap curtains over them, and the bottom of the trailer had a dark outside waterline. The front door had a green lumber porch built up in front of it with an overhang. Rain cascaded off the slanted porch roof in a waterfall so thick it could have drowned a hippopotamus wearing diving gear.

I bet it was nice inside. Probably an example of interior decorating at its best. Lots of deer heads and a couch covered in camouflage, a shit-ring around the toilet, and maybe some cumstained towels.

It was the only trailer on that lot, and it was set into a cutaway of the forest, which left it exposed out front and with trees at the back and on the sides. There was a pole with an automatic light on it, and it was on because the rainy sky had turned the world dark and soon the night would add to it.

In the glow of the light, I could see a small TV satellite dish on top of the trailer and I thought I recognized three struggling blades of grass on a patch of clay out to the side of the trailer along with some random spots of caliche.

In the caliche driveway, a soda-pop-orange truck was parked.

We spread out. I went left and Leonard went straight to the front door, hunkered down on the tacked-on porch. Pookie went right.

When I came around to the back of the trailer, I saw one window had open curtains. I ducked down under it and glanced over at Pookie coming up from the other side of the trailer. There was a door at the back of the trailer and a few steps leading up to it.

I met Pookie at the porch, and we got up close to the door and pressed our ears against it. We could hear a TV going. It was the usual twenty-four-hour redneck-news channel.

There was no overhang on the back porch and the rain came down on us like wet bullets. I was so miserable, I was ready to do something even if it was wrong.

I left Pookie where he was and went back to the window with the open curtains, lifted my head, and peeked inside. I could see George sitting on the couch with his shoes off, his socked feet up on a stool.

I edged back to Pookie, got out my lock pick, and went at it, silently as possible. In the meantime, Pookie sent Leonard a text letting him know what we were doing.

The lock snicked softly, and when it did, I jerked the door back, and Pookie and his pistol slipped inside.

37

George jumped to his feet as we came in, got caught up in the stool, and fell on his face. He started crawling toward the corner of the room where a shotgun leaned against the wall. I sort of accidentally stepped on his hand and stood on it with most of my weight.

He let out with a scream. By then Pookie had the shotgun.

I took my foot off George's hand, said, "Why don't you sit on the couch, partner."

He sat on the couch, which was not covered in the expected camouflage but had been nicely decorated in what appeared to be coffee, beer, and probably ejaculation stains. He sat there with his teeth gritted, holding his injured hand against his chest.

I picked up the stool George had tripped over, pulled it back a few feet from the couch, and sat down on it. Pookie gave me the shotgun. I placed it across my knees.

Pookie went over and turned on the light.

I looked around. There was indeed a deer head on the wall, and the nose of it looked to have been a moth buffet. One of the eyes looked as if it might fall out of the head. There was a cobweb in one nostril.

"What the fuck are you guys doing?" George said.

"We thought this was where the party was," I said.

"Fuck you," he said.

"Man, that told us off," I said.

"Yeah," Pookie said. "I feel told."

Pookie picked up the remote from the arm of the couch and cut off the TV racket, tossed the remote on the couch by George, then moved to the front door to let Leonard in.

Leonard came inside. He had been under the porch overhang, but he was still damp. He shook like a dog, slinging rain everywhere, including on me.

"You're the first nigger ever through that doorway," George said. "And you'll be the last."

"Yeah. You look like you're in a great position to give me shit."

Leonard sat in a fat-cushioned armchair and kind of worked his ass around on it.

"I'll burn that chair when you're gone," George said.

"Ought to burn this whole place down, way it looks," Leonard said. "I'd start with that fucking couch. What the fuck, man? All that money Jackie put in the bank, and you never got around to buying a nice place, and now she's gone, and you're left with dick, and I bet it's a little one."

"What money?" George said. But I could see his eyes had brightened with interest.

"Don't go dumb," I said. "Or dumber than usual, anyway. You were stealing money from Professor. If Professor found out, bet you told him Jackie stole it for Ace, since he ended up with it."

Of course, he hadn't actually ended up with it, but I thought that was a good place to start.

"Goddamn it," George said.

"Bet it hurts to think Ace was working his weenie in your gal's pussy," Leonard said. "Big, black wiggle-weenie. Even made a baby with her."

"That kid didn't last long," George said, and there was an odd look on his face. It looked a lot like the one he'd had when I stood on his hand.

"Here's the thing we're thinking," I said. "We have all of Jackie's accounting, how and where she put Professor's money. He may not even know yet it's missing, and the thing is, we got a clear trail to you, buddy. We can prove a lot of that money was in your account before it was in Ace's and then, later on, some-one else's."

"Someone else's?" George said. "Someone besides Ace?"

"Yeah," I said. "You didn't know about that. You knew about Ace because I bet she told you. Kind of a jab. That might be why she can't be found. You didn't like being made a fool of, though, frankly, George, I think you should accept fool as your full-time job."

"Wait a minute, now," he said. "I didn't do nothing to her."

"Remains to be seen," I said.

"Look here, I didn't know she was doing that," George said. "Not at first."

"And when you did," Leonard said, "you told her to put it back in Professor's account. Want us to believe that?"

"Sure. I didn't want that money."

"I call bullshit on that," Pookie said. "I think you'd steal quarters off a dead man's eyes."

George jerked his head toward me. "Who the hell is this plug?"

"He's going to be the plug that sticks that pistol in your ear and gets rid of about forty years of ear wax," Leonard said.

I could see that George had gone from being frightened to being terrified. And I don't think it was the gun threat that was doing it.

"Thing is, your fault, Jackie's fault, the fault in the stars," I said, "doesn't make a lot of difference. I think you try and explain to Professor how you didn't know it was going on, that'll be like kicking a dead rabbit and telling someone it's jumping."

Sweat beads popped on George's forehead. Outside, thunder rolled and the rain came down harder than before, spattering on the cheap mobile-home roof. Loud enough I had to speak up.

"Know what I think?" I said. "I got an idea you did use some of that money, maybe laying you out a getaway plan, and Jackie might not have gotten away with it all."

"Yeah," Pookie said, "wouldn't it be funny if some of it traced to a nice house and truck somewhere. Probably in another state."

"Never did nothing like that," George said.

"Let me get right to it," I said. "You need to tell us about Jackie, where she is—"

"I got no idea," he said.

"Don't interrupt my man when he's talking," Leonard said.

"Like I was saying. You tell us what we want to know, and we won't tell Professor what you don't want him to know."

George hung his head.

"Goddamn it," he said. "Jackrabbit said we could bleed off more money. To wait. We'd be filthy rich. I didn't buy anything. I don't have a goddamn thing waiting anywhere. Don't even own the junkyard. Professor, he bled me off, said he was helping me. I wanted to pay a bill, I had to go to him to get permission. I worked for that son of a bitch for years, and that's the thanks I got. I wanted to fuck him over by taking some of his money. And I was sick of those goddamn twins. Always sneaking around."

"That's a sad fucking story," Leonard said.

"Jackrabbit said we would take the money and go, and then after a time she quit hanging around with me and I started getting pissed, and then I find out she's fucking Ace, and then I wanted my money, or my share, anyway, and I wanted rid of her."

"I bet you wanted rid of Ace too," I said.

"Sure," George said. "Then I found out the accounts she made for me, they were empty. Every cent. There wasn't even electricity left in those online accounts. I told Professor that I didn't trust Jackrabbit, said he ought to have someone look at his books. That was my way of getting back at her. He hired some smart-ass from Houston to give the records a check and saw how his money had been shifted. But me, I was in the clear. Ace had the dough by then. Professor never knew I had it, way I figured it."

"We found her records," I said. "And they will show you had that money for some time. It will be hard for Professor to believe you didn't have a clue. We could explain to Professor what you did and just walk away. How will that work out for you? I think those twins will be paying you a visit. It might be best to give us all the information there is to give, because you might end up with the cops, and they like you better when you're cooperative."

I let him mull that over.

"Of course, me and Leonard, we're not law. We can do what we think is best."

"Yeah," he said, "and how good will your best be?"

"It's what you got," I said. "We're it, Georgie."

"I tell you some things," George said, "you got to protect me best you can."

"Sure," I said.

It hurt me a little to know I was telling a lie.

38

I looked at Pookie, said, "It might be time for you to go."

Leonard got up, walked over to Pookie, and said, "You go on back to the bed-and-breakfast. You can't be here. Some things the law can't see and still be the law. We'll catch up to you later."

Pookie looked hesitant.

"I mean it," Leonard said.

Pookie nodded. He and Leonard touched hands, and out Pookie went.

"He's with the law?" George said. "You said no law."

"He's gone now," Leonard said, and he sat down in the armchair again.

"Tell us something we don't know," I said to George. "For that matter, tell us some things we do know, but don't get cute. Don't try and beat around the bush."

You could see George's brain weighing the possibilities, and then you could see him give in.

"Like I said, I told Professor about the scam Jackrabbit had going, like I had found it out and was turning her in because I wanted to save him his money, money Ace had. I was also mad about the kid. I thought it was mine when she got pregnant. She didn't tell me otherwise. I thought she was going to the library, turned out she'd been fucking Ace. I was thinking I was going to be a father, and I was getting used to the idea. Then one day she doesn't come to work, and then the money is gone out of my account. I find out about Ace, and then the baby's born and it's black as motor oil. Seen her and it around town a time or two. I didn't want nothing to do with her then, but I won't kid you, I was mad about that money too."

"And that's when you told Professor," I said.

"Professor decided it wasn't going to stand, him being snookered, and by a woman with a nigger baby. No way. You got to understand, he talks smooth, but you fuck with him, he'll jerk a knot in your dick. Or he'll have someone do it for him. The twins or someone else. One night, she's off to the store, her and that kid, and Professor has them nabbed on the way out."

"By you?" Leonard said.

"No. I couldn't do that. I didn't like what she'd done, that kid and all, and I hated Ace, but I couldn't do that, knowing what he was going to do. Anyway, Professor had done what he had done. He told me I could have Ace. I followed him one night to her old place, snuck up on him, grabbed the back of his jacket, jerked him down, and killed him with a Boy Scout hatchet. Those motherfuckers are sturdy."

"About Jackie and the kid?" I said. "What did he do to them?"

"Can I have a smoke?" he said.

"Light up," I said.

He scrounged around in his shirt pocket and pulled out a pack of smokes, shook one out, and lit it with a lighter he had in the same pocket.

"Professor had her and the kid brought out to the hog farm."

"And you're saying you weren't there?"

George shook his head briskly. "No. No way. But Professor and Red both told me about it. He had Red and the twins throw the kid to the hogs, like it was hog food. It didn't take them hogs long, Red said. Hog, if it's hungry enough, can eat a body like a cheese sandwich, and a little body like that . . ."

George paused. He actually did look bothered. He took a deep drag on his cigarette.

"I'm glad I didn't see it," he said.

"Jackrabbit fed to the hogs too?" I said.

"No. They were going to, wanted her to see what happened to the baby as punishment, but when they did that, she tried to climb over the barrier and get to the child. They held her back. She fought like a tiger, Red said, managed to break loose and get away. Baby was ripped apart by that time. She got through the woods out there and they couldn't find her, and then Jackrabbit wasn't around anymore. I think if they got her, they'd have said. They both told the same story.

"Professor don't normally do his own shit work, or even be around it, but that night, he was there. What happened out there to that kid. Not my style."

"I think something like that could get to be your style," Leonard said. "Cowards can go any kind of way the wind pushes them."

George turned his head, looked at Leonard. "I think I could take you. I don't think you're so tough. Ace, now, he was tough."

"With you sneaking up behind him with a hatchet, you never

really got to find out," Leonard said. "I did find out, and I handed Ace his ass. And without a hatchet."

"Sure you did," George said.

Neither Leonard nor I said a word. We just looked at him. I saw George's face change.

"Want to take on the man who whipped Ace's ass?" Leonard said. "You up for that? Maybe I ought to give you a hatchet to even things out."

Leonard gave me the pistol and stood up.

"Oh yeah, you're going to play it tough," George said, "but you got your boy here with my shotgun."

"He ain't going to do nothing but keep the peace in case you decide to run. I think that's a possibility."

George's face darkened.

"You want to talk tough, now I give you the chance to be tough," Leonard said. "You're still going to end up with the cops, but before that, you're going to get a beating."

"You said no cops."

"We lied," I said.

"You can't do that," George said.

"What do you think this is?" I said. "A sport?"

"Here's what you can get out of this deal, George," Leonard said. "And it's all you're likely to get, and it ain't that likely. You beat me, you get that satisfaction. I beat you, I get that satisfaction. Whatever, you still end up in a jail cell. And I tell you right now, you want to fight or you don't, you're going to take a beating."

George looked at me.

"What he said," I told him.

"Why?" George said.

"We don't like you," I said.

"No, we don't," Leonard said. "You need to take better care of dogs."

"What?" George said.

"You heard me," Leonard said.

"You took Rex, didn't you?"

Leonard merely smiled at him.

"Sure you want to bother with this?" I said to Leonard.

"Right now, it's all I want to do," Leonard said. "Get up, cracker, you and me are going to dance a bit."

George stood up slowly, dropped the cigarette on the carpet, and put it out with his sock-covered heel. I guess he was showing us how tough he was. He was certainly a big boy. His mouth twisted in a smile as he gave Leonard a hard look. It wasn't that confident a smile or a look, actually. Fear lived behind that mask.

Leonard locked the front and back door and moved to the center of the room. He stretched slightly to get the kinks out, bent his head from one side to the other. When he did, his neck made cracking sounds.

"Yeah," Leonard said. "Now I'm good."

George eased to the center of the room with Leonard, his hands up.

I kept my place on the stool.

George went for it, let one loose, a big looping right. If it had made solid contact, it could have dropped an ox, but making contact is the trick.

Leonard ducked the meteor, and then he was in on the bigger man, striking a series of quick punches low and to the kidney and bladder. George made a huffing sound, and then he hooked a left, and that caught Leonard, but Leonard turned with it. He'd have a bruise, but no bones were broken.

George came with a series of them now. Leonard slipped or ducked them all, and then he opened up.

George was easy. He was nothing. He was free pie.

Leonard worked the body so hard and fast, George couldn't put any punches together, not anything good, anyway. And when he bent low to cover the spots Leonard was hammering, my man opened up on George's face with a series of fast uppercuts. Leonard might as well have had a meat cleaver in his hand or that hatchet George had used, way he was cutting George up.

George staggered forward, tried another looping right, missed. Leonard slipped under it and to the side and swung a left deep into George's belly. George dropped down on his ass. Leonard kicked him in the face and knocked him on his back. George peed himself. It was an acid smell and the piss stained George's pants and the carpet.

George acted like he was going to try and get up, but then he shook his head, said, "No more," and laid out on his side, breathing hard.

"You are one of the easiest nuts I ever cracked," Leonard said.

That's when headlights shone through the dingy curtains.

39

Not the newspaper boy, I assume," Leonard said.

"Think it might be our dear friends Jimmy and Lou," I said.

"I been wanting to see them again," Leonard said.

George lifted his head, said, "You son of a black bitch."

"Most likely," Leonard said.

"George," I said, "you move, I'll shoot you."

"I'm laying in piss," he said.

"And whose fault is that?" I said.

I was looking out the gap in the curtains as I talked to George.
I saw two men get out of the pickup. Yep. Jimmy and Lou. You
could tell Jimmy right off, the way he held his head, as if someone
had screwed it on crooked.

They had what looked like shotguns.

Not good.

Leonard slipped to the other side of the door where there was
another window, pushed back the curtains, and looked.

"Maybe I need to get my pistol back," he said.

"My pistol," I said.

"Tomayto, tomahto," he said. "Besides, you got the shotgun."

He walked briskly over to me and took the pistol.

That's when we heard the back door of the trailer swing open, and George was out of there in his sock feet.

"Goddamn it," Leonard said. "I must be losing my touch. I hit him really hard."

"Lock the doors," I said.

Leonard did that. I saw George out the front window, coming into view. He had come around the trailer, moving awkwardly, nursing his kidneys. He had his hands above his head, waving frantically at Jimmy and Lou.

"It's me," he called to them. "It's me."

Jimmy spoke over the rain.

"I know who you are."

And then Jimmy and Lou lifted their shotguns and fired. The blasts hit George and tore him up. Little dark spots jumped from his body and disappeared beyond the glow of the yard light. George hit the ground so fast, it looked like a circus trick.

Lou walked over to him and shot him in the head, just in case there were still a couple of brain cells stirring.

Jimmy called out to the house, "Hap. Leonard. Know you're in there. Why don't you come out and let's get this over with?"

Leonard gently unlocked the front door and cracked it open.

"Hell no. It's nice and cozy in here, except for the stink where George pissed himself. Why don't you come in and have a cup of my black ass, you crook-neck shit-ass?"

Jimmy grinned wide.

"You done hurt my feelings, talking about my neck. Don't be a coward. Come out."

"Don't be an idiot," Leonard said. "You boys come on up in here and get us. Let me see I can straighten that neck out for you."

"That's the way it's got to be, we can come on up in there," Jimmy said.

"Can you?" Leonard said. "Well, come on in. The bullets are fine."

Jimmy turned and trotted back to the pickup. He and Lou got inside, and Jimmy gunned it.

The crazy bastard was racing straight for the trailer.

40

The truck was flying right at my position at the window.

I did a kind of quickie two-step and dived across the room. That's when the truck hit the trailer and there was a loud collision, like the heavens blowing a bean fart. The window glass was knocked out, the window frame caved in, and the front of the truck came inside the mobile home. A light fixture fell from the ceiling, crashed on the floor near me, and the home heaved off its foundations and dropped on one end, sent me sliding with Leonard tumbling after me.

I lost the shotgun for a moment, and then I had it again. I almost managed to get to my feet, but unless I was a fly, I wouldn't have been able to actually stand, so I fell to the ground on my belly, rolled to the side, pumped one into the sixteen-gauge chamber.

The mobile home was still moving but in slow motion now as it continued to swivel off its foundation blocks. The lights went out, except for the light on the post outside and the truck lights that were shining right at me; they lit the inside of the home pretty well.

I heard Leonard behind me cussing.

I glanced back. He had rolled into the bedroom door and knocked the hinges off, loosened up a plastic fuck doll from somewhere. It lay across his back where it had fallen, as if trying to mount him. Leonard still had the pistol in his hand.

I heard the truck doors slam, and then Jimmy appeared on the hood of the truck, which was poking through the remains of the window like an anteater's nose. He was standing there with his head at that odd angle, like he was being inquisitive. His shotgun roared, and as I was in a precarious position, he had me, but that's when the sagging mobile home slipped completely off the blocks and fell, throwing off his aim. The shotgun blasted the wall behind me. The home dropped hard, and when it hit the ground, the impact sent Jimmy flying off the hood and into the home, banging him up against the couch, which was slow-sliding across the floor.

The drop jarred my teeth, but now the home was mostly flat on the ground. I came up on my knees as Jimmy, still clutching the shotgun, tried to regain his composure. I didn't let him. Here's a tip in life-or-death struggles: Unlike the Lone Ranger, you don't shoot guns out of people's hands. You shoot them solid and you shoot to kill, and a shotgun in that situation is sweet.

I cut down on Jimmy just as he was about to cut down on me. He wasn't more than ten feet from me, maybe less. My blast was first, and when he was hit, his shotgun rode up and fired into the ceiling.

I thought for an instant I could see light through Jimmy, but it could have been an illusion. His crooked head even straightened slightly, and then he toppled onto his face and his butt went up in the air and wiggled a bit, and then he came down on his stomach, squirmed like a snake on a hot stove, then went still. Debris from the ceiling sprinkled him like snow.

His head had fallen so that his chin was supporting him. His eyes were looking right at me. I felt as if I saw his life wing its way out of him, through his eyes and into the shadows, like frightened quail scattering into the brush.

Leonard was on his feet now, stepping past me.

Lou was entering through the window with his shotgun. When he saw Jimmy's dead ass, he made a noise. It was a cold and horrible sound, like a rabbit dying. Before Lou could get a bead on either of us, Leonard let off a shot from the pistol.

I couldn't tell where the shot hit Lou, but I heard a smacking sound and saw dark liquid fly up, momentarily framed by the pole light outside; the drops seemed to fall in slow motion.

Lou went sideways at a stumble, through the gap in the wall, back onto what remained of the hood of the truck, which looked like an accordion pushed in. The crunch in the hood caught his foot, and he fell, toppled out of sight.

Like a juggernaut, Leonard went after him, springing through the gap and onto the hood. I heard a shot from the handgun. I came out right behind Leonard, and when I got there, Lou was running toward the road, wobbling. He had dropped the shotgun.

Leonard jumped off the truck and walked after Lou like the angel of death about to collect a soul. The rain was still coming down.

Lou stumbled and fell. He fell hard. He started to crawl, clawing his fingers into the wet dirt.

I came up quickly behind Leonard, and now Leonard was right on top of Lou. He lifted the pistol. I gently pushed it aside.

"No need for that," I said.

Lou was still crawling.

"Maybe I ought to pop him one for mercy," Leonard said.

"I don't think you're feeling all that merciful," I said.

"You're right. I just want to pop him."

"Leave the poor bastard be," I said.

The decision was taken out of our hands as Lou shivered slightly and quit crawling. He collapsed slowly, lay with his face in the wet dirt, let out his breath, and was as still and silent as his brother.

In the distance, we could hear dogs and coyotes howling, disturbed from their nightly activities by the sounds of our gunfire, and most likely the stench of death.

41

Delf said, "Dead? Both of them?"

"Yeah," Leonard said.

"They tried to kill you?"

"Yeah," Leonard said.

Delf was sitting behind his desk in the police station. Me and Leonard and Pookie were standing in front of his desk. We had already told him the story of what George had told us, how his brothers died.

"How again, exactly?" Delf said. He looked so stunned, so sad, it was painful.

"We're sorry," I said, but I didn't tell it to him again.

"Jesus," he said.

Eula came in from the front desk and rolled a chair over next to Delf, put her hand on top of his, which was lying on the desk like a dead bird.

"I knew it was coming, I guess," Delf said, "I even thought you guys being in town might lead to it. I should have encouraged you not to come back."

"We had no choice," I said.

"And why were you not there?" Delf said to Pookie.

"I'm an officer of the law, same as you. I couldn't take a confession illegally. Hap and Leonard could. It's worth what it's worth to a jury, but I didn't want any part of it. I didn't know your brothers were going to show up or I would have stayed. I think it would have come out the same way."

Delf shook his head.

"Oh Jesus. I'm glad Mother isn't alive. She would be devastated. Christ, I'm devastated."

"Again, sorry," I said.

Leonard had not said sorry once. The reason he hadn't was he wasn't sorry. He could kill you and sleep like a baby if he'd felt he had to do it, felt you had it coming. He thought a lot more people had it coming than I did.

The door opened and Johnny walked in. He leaned against the wall with his arms crossed. Like Eula, he had heard the story earlier, when we reported it. They had called Delf at home, had him come in.

"I guess we need a formal statement, and then I got to go look at the crime scene," Delf said.

"I sent what passes for our forensic team out there," Johnny said. "You don't need to see that shit, Chief."

"Yeah," Delf said. "Maybe not."

Delf's face looked as if he had just bit into alum, and suddenly he got up from behind the desk and came around quickly, heading right at me, as I was the closest. Johnny grabbed him and turned him and guided him like a child back to his chair. Delf sat down and put his head in his hands.

"Did you have to kill them?" he said through his fingers.

"Yep," Leonard said. "That's getting to be an old question. It was us or them. They came to kill George, and did, and when they saw our car, knew we were there, they thought they'd get a three-fer."

"If it's any consolation," I said, "Jimmy died like a man."

"It isn't," Delf said. But then he dropped his hands and looked at Leonard. "Lou. Did he die well?"

"No one dies well," Leonard said. "I gut-shot him twice. I meant to kill him right off but didn't. I won't kid you. I wanted to shoot him again when he crawled away from us like a fucking snake in the grass. And let me warn you, you get up to hit me or Hap, law or no law, I will knock you down."

"Hey," Johnny said, and moved away from the wall.

"Take it easy," Pookie said. "I have to knock you down and Leonard knocks Delf down, it'll be hard to move around in this little room."

"You boys quit posturing," Eula said.

Johnny and Pookie exchanged glances, then Johnny leaned back against the wall. Pookie stood where he was, didn't bat an eye or move a muscle.

"Delf asked how Lou took it," Leonard said. "And I told him."

"I did," Delf said. "I did indeed. What I'm going to do is ask Johnny here to take you two to the interrogation room. Officer Carroll, you are free to go."

"I'd rather stay," Pookie said.

"Have it your way," Delf said. "Johnny will see all of you get coffee."

"No, I won't," Johnny said.

42

In the interrogation room we sat without coffee at the table where we had sat before. Johnny was standing, leaning against the wall in the same way he had leaned against the wall in Delf's office. Pookie was leaning against the opposite wall. Johnny and Pookie studied one another from time to time, sizing up who had the biggest dick, I guess, and who could swing theirs the hardest.

"You had to kill those two assholes?" Johnny said to us.

"On a loop here," Leonard said.

"Damn," Johnny said, shaking his head. "Sure. Sure. I know they had it coming. I know that. Just don't like seeing Delf like that."

"Then quit asking us about it," Leonard said. "Do what you're going to do. Charge us. Send us home. Fuck us in the ass and call us Daisy, but ask any more questions, we call a lawyer. We got a good one named Veil. Course, we'll have to fly him in from Oregon."

"There'll be questions, but not by me," Johnny said. "Not any-more. Ah, hell. It could just as easily have been me. I thought once they were going to go for me. I saw them and they saw me one time out by the old spillway. I wasn't on duty. I was fishing. I thought they were going to take me out, way they looked. They had guns with them, wearing them on their hip. Ain't that shit when the law allows that and they aren't law or military? Can you imagine a coincidence like that? Me there and them there."

"Me and Hap believe in coincidences," Leonard said.

"I don't. I think they came to kill me. They didn't have any fishing gear. I had my police-issue with me, and I guess they decided the time wasn't right. Or maybe they got cold feet."

"Jimmy didn't seem like the cold-feet type," I said. "Just cautious."

"Maybe it was a coincidence. Perhaps they had come to fish. If they had, they never did, not near me, anyway. For all I know they didn't leave, just went downstream to fish away from me."

"In our case, tonight was a coincidence," I said. "They happened to find us with George, and I think Professor sent them to take care of a loose end. I think Professor knew George was a weak link, knew he had been stealing money. Knew he knew some things he wished he didn't know. We would have been icing on the cake, had they been successful."

"Been those twins, might have been a different story," Johnny said.

"We hear about them," Leonard said, "but far as we know they haven't done shit."

"A lot of it might be hot air," Johnny said, "but a lot of it might not be. I vote on the side of caution."

"Do you know their names?" I said.

"Yeah. The twins."

"Nice," I said.

"That's all I got, all anyone knows. Word is they have done quite a bit of killing, but the problem is that's all we got, a word or two. Again, I stick on the side of caution, just in case they're as badass as some say they are."

Delf stuck his head in the door, said, "All right, boys. Going to see the Professor. Going to give him a bit of a talk. I'm bringing you with me."

"Really, Delf?" Johnny said. "I mean, Chief. That isn't protocol."

"It is tonight," Delf said. "I'm the goddamn police chief of this one-horse town, and if I say they go, they go. And Officer Carroll here, I'm temporarily deputizing him in our jurisdiction so he can go with us."

"Can you do that?" Johnny said.

"I'm the goddamn police chief, didn't you hear?" Delf said. "Consider yourself deputized, Officer Carroll. Town council can fire me if they like. Right now I wish they would, but for tonight I'm still the boss, and I'm calling in everyone, off duty or not. Saddle up, boys, let's go. Now. I have a judge to see first, and then we will give Professor an antisocial call."

43

Killing people makes you tired. It erodes your soul as well. In Leonard's case, I think it might energize him, but me, right then, I was feeling worn out and blue with a soul as thin as the edge of a razor. I didn't seem to know anything anymore. I was like a student at the Helen Keller School of Astronomy for the Blind, looking through a telescope. It was dark out there.

Me and Leonard were sitting in the back of the cruiser Delf was driving. Pookie and Johnny were in another.

My cell rang. It was Brett. She gave me some info and I told her I was kind of in a bad spot and had to go. When I turned off the cell, I said, "Here's something else. Computer guy, he found out something about all this money Jackie has been moving. Librarian, Cinner, that was supposed to have got all the money? Well, she didn't really get all the money either. Jackie made it look like Cinner had the money. It was in accounts that seemed to point to her, but our man looked closer, saw they were shells, that the money was offshore."

"Damn," Leonard said. "I hate fucking computers. How can you make something look one way and it be something else? It gives me the heebie-jeebies."

"Guess whose name the money was really in, when it was all said and done. Guess who had all the money?"

"What the fuck is this?" Delf said, slowing the car a little. "A quiz show? I'm not in the mood for this shit. Just tell me."

"Professor," I said. "Guy who supposedly was being snookered and had lost all the money suddenly had all the money, and maybe he had it all along, slipped it through other accounts like shit through a goose. Money-laundering it somehow. Getting it off-shore. It was a shell game. Everyone thought the peanut was under their shell, but thing was, Professor always had all the peanuts."

"It do be confusing for a simple country boy," Leonard said. "Seems to me, Jackrabbit would have had to do that for him."

"Maybe he forced her to do it," I said.

"Well, one thing we need are any computers Professor might have," Delf said.

Professor's place wasn't as fancy as you might think for a man with money. It was a large acreage with a number of storage buildings on it, and the house was good size but looked to have been designed by an idiot. You could see sections had been built onto it randomly, like the Winchester House but without the class. It even had one little stained-glass window, high up on the left side. I couldn't make out the design because no light came from behind it, but it was the only piece of stained glass visible.

Before we drove out, Delf had managed to quickly get a search warrant from a judge, went directly to his house, telling him something or other. We had to wait in the car like children while he was inside.

Now we were at the Professor's pad with Delf and his search warrant. Johnny and Pookie were already there in the other cruiser. They had come through the open gate the same as we had. It wasn't locked. Frankly, it wasn't much of a compound and it wasn't well kept.

There was a big white man with a tavern tumor sitting in a lawn chair on the front porch. The overhang was running with rainwater, and some of it was splashing on him, but he had on a rain slicker with a hood. He looked uncomfortable. Another big fellow, also a white guy, also in a rain slicker, was in the yard, wandering about like a child looking for Easter eggs. He came out of the shadows and was partially lit up from a yard light.

They both had weapons, rifles of some sort. The man in the lawn chair stood up. There was a feeling in the air like the last bridge had washed away and the dam was about to break.

It intensified as another cop car arrived and two black men got out of it, one short and fat, the other lean and tall. They would be the off-duty guys Delf had called in. They had on slickers and they stood by their cars in the rain. They had pushed their slickers back so they could rest their hands on their guns.

Delf, Pookie, and Johnny went up to the door to serve the search warrant. The other two cops didn't move. The man walking around with the rifle stopped moving. This was the time when things could go wonky, shots could be fired, people could be killed. Leonard and I slowly got out of the car and stood in the rain. I didn't want to be trapped in that damn car.

Still, I felt kind of helpless standing out by the cruiser with no real power to do anything but put my hands in my pockets and hold my balls and let the rain run over me. Even with the rain like that, in the strong wind you could smell the hog farm that was out back of the house, near the woods. As we'd driven up, we could see the shape of it back there, huge and ominous, pigs getting fat. I wondered if they knew they were going to die for someone's bacon.

As Delf, Pookie, and Johnny reached the porch, the man in the lawn chair stood up and blocked Delf. He was much bigger than Delf.

We could hear them clearly while they talked.

"Belvin," Delf said, "are you really going to try and block a sworn officer of the law and someone who's known you since you were small enough to shit in diapers?"

"Nothing personal, Delf," Belvin said.

Johnny was standing off to the side of the porch, his hand on his gun. His dark skin and the black of the gun blended as if they were one.

Pookie was standing away from both of them, watching the man in the yard. Pookie had his hand behind his back. He was holding the butt of his pistol where it rested in a holster fastened to his belt.

The other man came wandering in from the yard. He held his rifle in an obviously nonthreatening manner.

"Ah," Delf said to the man as he walked up, "Terry Joe Fisher. Son of a bitch. I didn't see it was you. Weren't you preaching somewhere?"

"Not enough in the offering plate," he said. "Had to quit it. I guess I wasn't called by God after all. For a while I was called by insurance, but I couldn't sell enough, and then there was real estate, but I wasn't any good at that either. So now I'm here."

"Listen here," Delf said. "You two, you all behind the Professor's shit?"

"Just hired guns," Belvin said. "Your brothers do the heavy lifting, and those two weird fucks and Red, until he got himself chewed up by a dog or some such."

"Jimmy and Lou have joined Red at the hog farm in the sky," Delf said. "Though not by dog bite. By bullet."

"Oh," Belvin said. "Oh, man. We didn't know."

"It was all of a sudden," Delf said.

"Where's Professor?" Johnny said.

"We got no idea if he's in there or not," Belvin said.

"Now, that's not true," Terry Joe said. "He's in there, and we both know it."

"Goddamn it, Terry Joe," Belvin said.

"I ain't going to talk shit that will get me in a hole," Terry Joe said. "And I wouldn't shoot nobody nohow. Thought I'd just have to walk around with a rifle and listen to Professor's bullshit and pick up a check. I ain't no better at this than I was at preaching, insurance, or real estate. I'm thinking maybe my calling is selling used cars or some such. I'm going home, if that's all right, Delf?"

"You go on, then," Delf said. "You go on, and that's the last friendly thing I do. I lost two brothers tonight, and, worse, they both had it coming. But it puts me in a mood. You feel me, boys? You feel my mood?"

"I feel you," Terry Joe said.

Hell, I could feel that mood all the way back at the car.

Terry Joe leaned the rifle against the doorsill on the porch and walked to where it was darkest at the edge of the house. A moment later we heard a car door slam, then there were lights, and then a truck came barreling around the left side of the house and was gone up the road faster than you could say, "Shit in a can and clamp the lid down tight."

The car's red taillights glowed back at us through the rain.

"What about you, Belvin?" Delf said.

"Professor has the note on my house and truck," Belvin said.

"Let me worry about that," Delf said.

"How worried will you be?"

"Quite worried."

"You'll do something?"

"What I can. Go home, have a beer, watch some TV. Jerk your dick, let the dog lick your balls."

"I could do that, couldn't I?" Belvin said.

"Either that or I'm going to knock your ass down, and if you lift that rifle, Johnny will shoot you."

"Two or three times," Johnny said.

"What am I going home to?" Belvin said. "Wife left me."

"Right sorry to hear that," Delf said, "but you got that dog I mentioned."

"Died," Belvin said.

"Hell, didn't you used to have a donkey? You could go home to the donkey."

"Ah, Delf, I was sixteen," Belvin said. "You know I don't own a donkey no more."

"Belvin here got caught putting the pork to a donkey's ass in a barn, standing on a bucket behind it."

"Sweet, sweet donkey love," Pookie said.

"Ah, goddamn it, Delf. People have mostly forgot about that. You didn't need to bring it up. 'Sides, that donkey died before the dog."

Pookie made a nickering sound like a donkey.

"That's not funny," Belvin said. "No call for that."

"Belvin," Delf said. "It's time for you to go. You can drive home and sit in the dark and dream about that long-dead donkey, or you can think about it in a jail cell. Make a choice, and make it now."

Belvin sighed, put his rifle where Terry Joe had put his.

Delf said, "Anyone in there with him?"

"Them twins are never far away," Belvin said.

"Go on, then," Delf said.

Belvin took a deep breath and walked into the darkness and around the corner of the house. Pretty soon there were headlights like before, then a white car, then there were only the taillights, and then like his partner, Belvin was gone.

"If only he had that donkey to go home to," Pookie said.

44

Del turned and waved the other two cops to him, then he looked at us. "Ah, hell, boys, quit leaning on the car. Come on over here, you're deputized."

We walked over to the porch. Delf handed us the rifles the guards had left.

"Prefer you just look threatening," Delf said. "Try not to shoot anybody. I don't want to have to explain this deputy thing too much, but some asshole in there, the twins, Professor himself, anyone that decides to channel their inner Wild Bill Hickok, shoot the shit out of them."

Delf pounded on the door and stepped off to the side.

No one answered.

"Johnny," Delf said. "You up for kicking it down?"

"Let me," Pookie said.

Pookie pulled his pistol out from under his shirt. He was preparing to kick the door when a shotgun blast tore through the door and hit Pookie solid in the chest and dropped him like Newton's apple.

45

The world got slow and I felt as if I were moving through gelatin. When the blast knocked Pookie down, his gun went up in the air, and it seemed to defy gravity, appeared to be floating down toward the earth with all the speed of a feather in an updraft. Along with it, fragments from the door spun in the air and were caught in the glow of the porch light.

And then the falling gun smacked on the concrete porch floor, spun a little on impact, and time came unstuck.

Leonard grabbed Pookie under the arms, pulled him off the porch and into the rain, back toward the patrol car. I could hear Pookie gasping like a large fish out of water. Leonard was saying, "It's all right, gonna be all right."

Johnny leaped across the porch and kicked the door. It cracked loudly, slammed hard against the wall, and sagged on one hinge.

Then Johnny, me, and Delf were inside. I could hear the two cops splashing in the rain after us, and then we were all inside, stupid-like, standing at the end of a hallway, trapped like a pack of rats in a sewer pipe.

In that moment fear washed over me and I could imagine someone stepping out with a shotgun, firing, smacking several of us in a scattergun blast.

There were two doorways at the end of the hall, and one to the right near us. I figured whoever had fired the shotgun had taken that closest exit, might be right inside, waiting, so you wouldn't want to go there. But I did anyway.

Can't explain a thing like that, but somehow, the idea of standing there, not doing anything, waiting for the other shoe to drop was worse than the idea of going through that open foyer and into whatever was beyond.

I went through at a crouch, the rifle in my hand, and when I came into the room, it was empty. In a strange way, I was disappointed. I wanted the bastard who had shot Pookie. I wanted him bad.

I edged back out into the hallway, and there was just me and Delf and Johnny now. I shook my head.

"I sent them around back," Delf said, referring to the two cops. "You can step out of this."

"Not likely," I said.

"Split up," Delf said.

I went back through the foyer and into the room as Delf and Johnny went down the hall, planning to split up and go into the rooms at the end, I figured, maybe right into a trap.

I moved along through the room, and then through an open door and into another hallway. I looked both ways down the hall and saw nothing. I was keenly aware of the sounds of the air conditioner humming and the rain slamming against the roof of the house.

Easing along, I came to a kitchen, and on the far side of it was an open door that led outside. There was a back-porch light and the rain made lines in the light beyond the porch like billions of falling needles.

I kept up my caution, glanced all about, but there was no trap. The kitchen was empty.

I made my way to the doorway and peeked around the edge of it and looked out at the night. There was too much light to see what was beyond it, and stepping out onto the back porch under the light would make me a perfect target. I touched the switch on the wall and turned off the light, eased through the doorway, staying low, and stepped off the porch. In the distance, I could see two shapes running toward a structure near the dark line of the woods back there. They were rushing toward the hog farm. I didn't know if it was the two cops Delf had sent out back or the twins. They were too far away and it was too dark to tell much about them.

I thought about alerting Delf and Johnny, but there could be other bad guys in the house with guns, and I didn't want to throw them off their diligence, so I took a deep breath and went out into the rain.

46

The hog farm was a long line of buildings linked together by brick and concrete, seemingly glued tight by thick shadows. Off the buildings was a stretch of pens made up of close-together horizontal bars covered over by an aluminum roof, and there were a handful of lights on high metal poles, and the lights shone down into the empty pens, which were floored with concrete. The smell of hog was thick in the air. The rain stirred the stench like a foul soup.

I didn't see the twins.

I didn't see the cops.

I didn't see any hogs.

The rain plastered my hair to my forehead. I had started to feel cold and uncomfortable. I glanced back at the house and thought maybe I should go back there and find reinforcements, but it wasn't a thought that stayed with me long. But one thing that did stick with me was the fact that the two cops could shoot me by mistake as easily as they could shoot the twins.

That was unnerving.

And then there was a blast that made me crouch, and I got a glimpse of gunfire at the far end of the pen, where it met the building. I saw a shape move quickly and gracefully from the side of the pen into the building, and I saw another shape fall out toward the pen.

I heard someone yell inside the building, and then I heard double shotgun blasts, and then a silence that was far from golden. I inched my way to the pen, slipped the rifle through the bars so that it was propped against them, stuck a foot on the lower bar, and climbed over.

I dropped down as silently as possible, picked up the rifle, and moved toward where the body had fallen. I was shaking a little, like leaves in a light wind.

I reached the wall of the building and put my back to it and crept along it until I came to where the man had fallen. There was enough light I could see it was one of the cops, even if his head was gone. He had on the uniform. His service automatic was still in his hand.

Trembling, I took the automatic from him and stuck it in my pants pocket, turned cautiously into the opening where the shape had gone, knowing now it had been one of the twins.

Inside it was dark and the smell was strong, but there was a light at the far end of the building, and I could see in the distance better than up close.

I crouched down and put my back to the wall and sat for a moment until my eyes adjusted to the darkness. I took a deep breath and started out along what I realized was a walkway. As I came nearer the light at the far end, I could see better. I could see the walkway was attached to a wall on the far side and ended at a closed door.

I also noticed that if I were to step too far left, I would fall into a long concrete trough, and worse, I would fall into what was in the trough. Manure and what might have been blood from butchering churning along, pushed by water, probably dropping off into a septic tank buried somewhere outside. It was hard to see exactly what was there in that light, but it was easy to smell and identify it. Right then I swore off sausage and pork chops but reserved the right to eat bacon.

If it wasn't bad enough that if I fell off the platform to the left I'd end up deep in hog shit and blood, to the right the concrete floor was twenty feet below, and it was my guess the hogs first entered there on their way into the butchering room. I could almost smell the remnants of their fear, or maybe that was my fear I smelled.

On I went, sweating, the rain pounding about the same rhythm as my heart. And then I tripped, lunged forward, almost lost my footing and fell into the hog mess, almost lost the rifle too, but I ended up keeping both. I got down on one knee and felt what I had tripped over.

I put my hand out and touched something soft and warm, wet and sticky. I pulled my hand back. I squinted. It was hard to see, of course, but I could make out that what I had put my hand in used to be a face. It was the body of the other cop, and he had fallen in such a way he was stretched across the ramp, barring the pathway.

I inadvertently wiped my hand on his uniform front, stepped over him, and moved toward the door. The twin who had killed him had to have gone through there, and now the door was closed, and if I were to open it, there was a good chance he, or both of them, would be waiting on the other side, ready to cut me in half.

I paused for a moment, then went back the way I had come,

outside the main building, under the aluminum hog-pen roof, and then over the side of the bars like before, only going outside this time. When I dropped on the other side and picked up the rifle, I could see the house in the distance, some of the lights on, and I thought I might ought to give it up and go back there.

But I didn't do that. I couldn't do that. The bastards had shot Leonard's Pookie.

I slipped around the outside of the building, ducking low where there were windows. There were a few dim lights inside, the kind that stay on all the time but have low wattage. I made my way on around the corner and got to the other side and saw a door there.

I didn't think going through a door was any better an idea now than it was before. I passed it and moved along the wall, came to a pen on the far side, only this one was filled with Yorkshire hogs. Rain splashed on the outside of the pen and hammered on the roof, and the hogs stirred restlessly down there, lots of them, too many for the space.

I put the shotgun through the bars, climbed over into a large pile of hogs, managed to pull the rifle out from under hog feet, picked it up, and made my way through them. It was like climbing over stinky, warm, moving boulders. They sniffed and honked. I tried not to excite them. I moved along there until I could see the pen had bars that led up to the side of the building, ended below a window. There was an orangish light in the window, like a candle inside a jack-o'-lantern.

With hogs bumping against me, one of them nipping painfully at the back of my thigh, I put the rifle against the bars and took off my shirt. I rolled it with a few whips of the wrist, then I tied one end to the rifle barrel, the other to the stock, making myself an impromptu strap. I slung the rifle over my shoulder with it, started climbing the bars by standing on a hog's head first, and inched my way up toward the window.

When I got up there, I peeked over the sill. It was a large window about the size of two normal ones, but it was one pane of glass.

In the orange light, I could see it was an office, and the pale-faced twins were in the center of it, standing back to back, at a slight crouch, facing the two doors I might have come through.

I hooked my right leg over a side bar, made myself as comfortable as possible, poked the rifle against the window glass gently, took aim, and was softly squeezing the trigger when one of the twins, perhaps alerted by a shadow, a sound, turned and saw me through the glass.

47

Any kind of weapon pointed at you is call for loose sphincter muscles, but a shotgun at that range is in a completely different league. As the twin whirled in my direction I fired my shot, but it was so hasty, I didn't know if I had hit anything, because the next thing that happened was I dropped the rifle and swung down with my legs caught up in the bar so that I was dangling upside down. I heard a clanking sound below me but didn't take time to note it. At the same instant, the glass was blown out by the shotgun and it rained down on me and the hogs below.

As I was trying to right myself and stay below that windowsill, out came the twin. I had just pulled myself up slightly when he leaned out of the window and poked the shotgun in my face. I grabbed the barrel and pushed it away from me, and that caused the twin to lose his balance and come tumbling out of the window and into the pen below.

He landed on some rambling hogs, and the shotgun bounced away from him and disappeared under a sea of hogs. I swung down on one of the bars and then leaped out at him as he tried to get up beneath a horde of now squealing and rampaging hogs. They ran together and knocked one another down and slid on the concrete that was wet from the blowing rain.

I dropped on a hog straddle-wise and rode it for a few feet before falling off. I turned at a crouch, and there came the twin. He had a knife he had produced from somewhere, and he was stepping partly on hog backs, partly on concrete, making a unique path in my direction.

I remembered the automatic I had picked up and reached for where I had shoved it in my pants pocket, and that's when I remembered the sound of something falling earlier, and now I knew what it was.

The twin stepped one foot up on a hog, and the hog moved, and the twin fell, and I tried to push my way through the hogs to him before he could get up, but that didn't happen. Just as I got to him, he was up and the knife slashed out at me.

I slap-passed it, but it got part of my naked skin, nothing terrible, but it seemed like a harbinger of things to come. I practice martial arts, have for years, including knife defense, but as my Shen Chuan instructor once told me, "There is no good knife defense, only a defense that is better than nothing."

Also, I had been stabbed and cut before and had found it most unpleasant.

The knife slashed back and I scooted back. It missed me by inches. He came again, a straight thrust this time. I grabbed his wrist with both hands, something my dad had taught me. I grabbed it and held on and kicked him in the nuts as hard as I

217

could. It was a little like kicking a Ken doll in the crotch. No effect.

He slugged me with his free hand, and it was a good left hook. It shook me. Birds and bees seemed to pass before my eyes, and hogs actually passed beneath my feet, and down I went, still hanging on to that wrist with both hands, pushing the blade away from me.

I wrapped my legs around him as a hog stepped on my face, and I could feel the wet stink against my naked back, the weight of the twin pressing down on me. He tried to slug me with his free hand again. I jerked my leg up and kicked him in the thigh and sent him back, and at the same time I squirmed out from under him, but I had lost my hold on his wrist.

He was up as quick as a whack-a-mole, and with the knife hand in front of him, his other hand folded across his chest to avoid me gripping it and to use it to slap punches I might throw, he advanced on me.

As he did, a hog ran between his legs and knocked him forward. I heard his teeth hit the concrete as two large hogs ran across his back. This caused his head to lift, and as it did, I kicked a field goal with it. It was a really hard kick, and I heard a sound like a rotten stick cracking, knew I had caused something to go in his neck. He made a noise like a water hose breaking loose, then lay flat on the concrete as more hogs walked on him. He was breathing, but barely. I could hear that busted sound still going, but softly now, like a child trying to play a bagpipe.

I shoved some hogs aside, searched about, found the twin's shotgun, decided that would do, and then, stumbling, nearly falling, I made my way toward the bars of the pen. I put the shotgun through them and climbed over, receiving a nip on the ass

218

from a hog as I went. Behind me, I could hear the twin making a sound almost like a scream caught up in a corked bottle and then I heard a sound like someone ripping a sheet, and I knew the hogs had him. He was still and bleeding, and now he was their sausage.

48

I worked my way around to the building again, and this time I decided to chance the door. I had done one of them in, so the one inside, if he was still there, couldn't be blocking both.

I tested the door. It was unlocked. I pulled it open quickly and slid inside at a crouch, my back against the wall. But no one was visible. I inched toward the desks, pointing the shotgun. No one was hiding between them. The door at the back of the room was wide open. I stood at the side of the door for a moment, looking out, letting my eyes become more accustomed to the light. The doorway led back the way I had come in originally, before I had turned around and gone back through the pen. It was a platform that jutted out onto the walk that bisected the trough of hog shit and the twenty-foot drop to a concrete floor.

I took a breath, went through the door, and that's when I knew he had me.

He was standing right there beside the wall, and as I came through he punched his shotgun against my temple, and in that instant I visualized all I was and all I would ever be flying away from me in blood drops, skull fragments, and brain matter.

But that's when Leonard, who had come up behind him, grabbed the shotgun barrel and jerked it up, causing a blast from the gun to smack loudly into the ceiling. He twisted the shotgun out of the twin's hand, said, "Give me that."

He used the stock on the surprised twin's head, twice in rapid succession, knocking him against the wall. Leonard crowded him so he couldn't fall, hit him again, flattening his nose. The twin staggered, and Leonard moved and let him stumble by.

Leonard put the shotgun against his head, pushed him with it, made him walk backward. Leonard said, "You don't fuck with Hap and Leonard, and I hope you're the one shot Pookie."

The twin looked at him oddly. A slight smile crawled across his otherwise dead face, and Leonard let her rip. The twin's head dissolved, and then he toppled into the hog shit. I went over for a closer look. He floated on top for a moment, and then the water moved him along, and he went under and churned out of sight.

49

Walking back to the house, I said, "Sorry about Pookie. He was a fine guy."

"Still is. He had on that bulletproof vest. He's got a bruise the size of a cantaloupe and the color of cancer on his chest, a few pellets in his face, some splinters from the door, maybe a cracked rib. Ambulance picked him up. He's at the hospital. He'll be all right."

"They killed both the cops," I said.

"I saw the bodies."

"You came at the right time."

"I usually do. You lost your shirt."

"Oh, really. I hadn't noticed."

Back at the house, Delf and Johnny were holding down the living-room couch.

"Sorry we weren't with you," Delf said. "We were clearing the house."

Leonard and I put the shotguns aside. "You did right," I said. And then I told them what had happened out there.

"It's messy," Delf said, "but you are deputies, and they were scum. We'll make it right. You lost your shirt, by the way."

"Oh, really."

"And you're bloody."

"Another surprise. What about the Professor?"

"Didn't find him," Johnny said. "But those dick guards said Professor was in the house. We were going to make another sweep for him or evidence."

Me and Leonard picked up our shotguns.

"Let's do this," I said.

50

The search was slow and tedious, and we didn't split up this time.

Delf and Johnny went through drawers and closets, everything, and me and Leonard followed about with our shotguns, just in case an army of samurai were crouched in a closet somewhere behind the winter coats.

You could see Delf and Johnny had already done this, way things were thrown around, but this time out they were less tender and short on police procedure.

At one point, Delf paused at one of the bathrooms and peed in the sink, us standing outside the open door, hearing his stream hit the porcelain. He came out drying his dick on a hand towel, which was not a pretty sight. He threw the towel in the corner and zipped up.

I said, "Doesn't that compromise evidence?"

"Not the way I see it," he said.

"All righty," I said.

Upstairs, Johnny took a leather jacket from a closet, tried it on. It didn't fit. "Shit," he said. "Always wanted one of these."

He tossed it back in the closet. It made a hollow sound when it hit the closet wall.

We searched high and low, but no Professor, and no real evidence. We ended up back in the living room.

"Could have slipped out the back way when we came up," Johnny said. "Might be why the twins were back there. He could be hiding with the hogs."

"He was, they'd squeal," I said.

"That's some funny shit," Johnny said. "But not that funny."

"Okay," Leonard said, "so we check the hog house, see if he's hiding there."

"I got to pee first," I said.

"Be sure and pee on something that matters, and wipe your pecker on a towel or curtain," Delf said.

"I saw the master at work," I said. "I know how it's done."

I didn't do that, though. I went to the toilet down the hall and took a leak, and when I finished, during the shaking of the member, I realized something.

I zipped up, went back to the living room.

"One thing," I said. "Outside, you look at the house, there's a room off to the top left. It has a stained-glass window. I don't remember seeing it from the inside."

"Oh," Delf said.

We all went upstairs, moved down a wide hallway to the far side of the house. We went into a room that should have been the room with the stained-glass window, but it only had a normal window.

I remembered that the closet where Johnny found the jacket

had only had a couple of coats in it, and I remembered too the sound it had made when it hit the closet wall.

The closet door had been left open. I turned on the light and stepped inside. The others stood outside the closet and watched me.

I ran my fingers along the left side of the closet. I could feel air blowing against my fingertips. I pushed gently against the wall, but nothing happened.

I took down the clothes bar to give me more room and felt around at the bottom of the drywall, but still nothing.

I heard Leonard say, "Here we go."

I came out of the closet and saw him touch the light switch. He pulled the switch down and turned off the light, then he turned the little panel that contained the switch. It moved easily. Under the light-switch panel was a gap, and you could see the wires that went to the switch, but you could see another switch inside.

Leonard hit the switch, said, "Open sesame."

The wall where I had felt the cool air made a snapping sound, and there was a bit of light shining through a crack.

Delf took out his pistol, went inside the closet, pushed the wall gently. It swung open.

51

In the room, you could see through the round stained-glass window, and you could see the rain blowing sideways in the light.

Johnny felt along the wall and found a switch, clicked it. The room filled with light. It was a bigger room than I'd expected. It was well furnished, even had a bed and a couch and a desk and a very fancy computer on it, along with a printer and a desk lamp. There was a door off to one side, a bathroom maybe.

I went over and opened that door gently, made sure I stepped back so no one in there with a gun would have a clear shot at me.

I peeked around the corner of the door, saw what was in there. Then we all saw what was inside.

In the bathroom, sitting on the pushed-down toilet lid, was a woman holding a dark-skinned baby sucking on a pacifier. The woman was dressed in blue jeans and a T-shirt. She was barefoot. She was very pretty, had black hair and prominent teeth.

"Not as good a hiding place as I had hoped," she said.

"Hey, Jackrabbit," Leonard said.

Johnny said, "Hey."

We turned and looked where he was looking. The bed. Underneath it we could see someone lying on the floor. Johnny walked over to the bed with his gun drawn.

"I am not armed," said the body from under the bed.

And then the body inched its way out into the open.

It was Professor.

52

We hustled Professor and Jackie downstairs, and Johnny went out to his car and brought me a T-shirt with a Marvel Creek Police Department logo on it. The logo was red. The shirt was blue, like me. I pulled it on. It was Johnny's size. You could have put two of me in it.

In the living room we all sat down, and I said, "So the baby wasn't fed to the hogs?"

Professor laughed. "You got that story from George. That's what he was told. What we wanted him to think. Look here, Delf, you see the baby is okay and Jackie is okay, so what's the problem?"

"My brothers aren't okay, and George isn't so good either. And you can add Red and the twins to the pile."

"The twins too?" Professor said.

"They weren't as bad as you thought," Johnny said.

"Oh, they were bad," I said, "just me and Leonard were more bad."

"They came with good recommendations," Professor said. "I paid them well. But just for protection. Nothing more."

Delf looked at Jackie. "What the hell?"

"We fell in love," Jackie said, and she gave Professor the sweetest look I have ever seen a woman give a man. It made my skin crawl.

"Black baby," Johnny said. "What gives, Professor? What about all that segregation shit?"

"I had a front to keep up," Professor said. "Without it, I'd lose influence."

"Professor doesn't care about color," Jackie said. "Not really."

"Jackie and me, we were a few days away from heading for someplace nice," Professor said.

"I got it," I said. "You and Jackie moved the money around so it wouldn't show you always had access to it. She's a whiz with numbers and computers, you're a con man. You don't believe in anything. You two took off—you three, actually—she and the baby would be thought dead, and you'd just be thought gone. That takes care of a lot of problems."

"Jackie changed me," Professor said. "That baby changed me. Boy's not mine, but it might as well be. I was selling all the hogs tomorrow. The farm. That was going to be the easy running cash."

"And you decided to tie up loose ends, like George," Leonard said.

"I didn't say that," Professor said. "Listen here. There's a lot of money. Let us go, you could end up with some of it. All of you."

"Write down he tried to bribe us," Delf said to Johnny.

Johnny didn't write down anything, but he nodded.

I looked at Jackie, sitting on the couch, the sleeping baby in her arms.

"I have a feeling the missing librarian didn't move off any-where," I said.

53

Leonard was home in LaBorde with Pookie on the day I went out to Miss Cinner's house with Delf and Johnny and a couple of men with shovels.

Delf and Johnny went through the place and found nothing outside of dust motes, a cutout section of carpet from the living room, and a damp smell in the kitchen.

The backyard was enclosed by a tall wooden fence. There was a scattering of flowers. The grass had grown up high, and it was especially high in one spot at the edge of the fence where the ground was slightly sunken.

Delf had a couple of minions dig there. While they did that, me and Delf and Johnny stood over them watching. Johnny even had his arms crossed. You would have thought we were important, way we stood there doing nothing.

"Funerals for the deputies tomorrow morning," Delf said. "You coming?"

"I'll be there. It could just as easily have been me," I said. "So, the twins?"

"Dug one out of the hog shit," Delf said. "The other one got pretty well eaten by the hogs, even the clothes got eaten, except for one shoe. I'm looking for an amputee that might need it."

"What's peculiar," Johnny said, "one in the shit, we took his fingerprints, and they're not in the system. We don't really know who they are and may never know unless DNA turns up something. I have a feeling it might not."

The diggers were at it about fifteen minutes before they found something. The missing patch of carpet. It was rolled and wrapped in duct tape. They cut the carpet loose of the duct tape and inside was a badly decomposed body. There was a ferocious stink about it.

We stood around the hole and looked down on what was inside.

Delf put his hands on his hips, crinkled his nose, said, "Miss Cinner, I presume."

54

It was late at night and I was back home in my own bed, having been to two funerals in one day. I was sleeping sound, all things considered, when Brett elbowed me awake and clicked on the lamp on her side of the bed.

"What?" I said.

"Don't sound unpleasant," she said.

"If you're waking me for sex, I forgive you," I said. "If not, I don't forgive you. I was dreaming I was Batman."

"It's not for sex, unless you really are Batman. Okay, here's the reason I woke you up. What's your favorite color?"

"What the hell?"

"Okay, your favorite number?"

"Jesus, Brett."

"Just fucking with you. Look here. I can't sleep. I got questions and need some answers. Let me get this straight. Jackie and Professor became partners?"

"You woke me for that?"

"Yep," she said. "She must have been something in the sack, to get him to give up his prejudice like that."

"Professor really fell in love with her, and he didn't care if she gave birth to a litter of rabbits. She got her hooks in him, and he liked it. Wouldn't surprise me if it didn't go both ways. He might have been next on her list to steal from. She might have even had plans to do him in."

"What about the librarian? Who killed her?"

"Could have been any of Professor's crowd, even her cousin Ace. Jackie was working everyone. Neighbors saw Jackie there, but after a point they didn't see Cinner. Appears Jackie took over the place. No telling what was done to Cinner to get her banking information. Miss Cinner thinks she's got a friend, and instead, she has the devil. I don't know. I'm guessing. We may never know."

"What about Sebastian?" she said.

"Again, no idea, same as when I got home. No revelations in my sleep."

"So that's it?"

"That's it. Hey, baby, now that we're awake, how about we try and reach the moon?"

"Are you asking to have sex?"

"Begging."

"No, thank you," she said, rolling over and turning out the light. "I'm sleepy now. Good night."

55

Couple days later, me and Brett and Leonard met the Mulhaneys at the office. We told them Jackie was in jail, told them
what had happened.

"I hate telling you this, but she told the chief over there that she
has nothing left for you two," I said. "And don't come see her in
jail."

Thomas looked sullen. Judith looked somewhere between sad
and relieved. She was very pale that day and seemed to have
turned frail.

"Thank you," she said. "Better to know than to not."

Leonard mentioned there was an outstanding debt for services
rendered. They smiled and left.

About a month after our meeting with the family, Jackie was released from jail. Professor copped to everything, said he forced
her to do what she did, and Jackie didn't argue against it. That got
her off the hook. I don't think anyone believed she was innocent.

They just couldn't prove she was guilty, not with Professor taking the rap like that, and I think her having that baby helped the court decide to let her go free and take care of the child.

But the topper came one afternoon when Brett got back to the house from shopping and said, "Did you hear?"

"Hear what?"

"In Marvel Creek, someone shot Jackie and her baby to death."

"What the hell? Wait a minute. What was she shot with?"

Brett shook her head. "A gun. That's all I know."

Not long after, Leonard came over. He had heard about it too.

"She was at the Professor's property, and someone broke in and shot her, and then the baby, who was in a bassinet. One shot to the head with a twenty-two for both."

I said, "Where did we first hear that probable scenario?"

"Thomas," Leonard said. "Come on. Drive me."

56

We rode over to the mobile home where Thomas lived with his mother. One end still had the tarp over it. There was a brand-new mobile home moved in next to it. The big truck was parked near the new home and it had a set of new tires on it and fancy hubcaps.

Driving up in the yard, we saw there was a black wreath on the door of the new trailer.

Leonard got out of my car and walked up the steps in front of the trailer's entrance and knocked hard on the door. I stood below the steps and rocked on my heels. The air was warm but still as death.

It took a while, but Thomas answered. He was wobbly and drunk and his pants were unzipped and his underwear was showing.

"What the hell do you want, nigger?" Thomas said.

Leonard grabbed Thomas by the throat so fast it was like a CGI effect. He pulled him out of the doorway of the mobile home and turned a little and sent Thomas hurtling over the steps and onto the ground.

Thomas started to get up. I said, "Stay there, if you know what's good for you."

"What the fuck is with you guys?" Thomas said.

Leonard went over and squatted near Thomas, who was in a half-lying, half-sitting position.

"Where's your mother?" Leonard said. "I don't mind she hears this."

"She died, had a heart attack a week ago, you black moron," Thomas said. "Why there's a wreath on the door. You ain't getting another cent from me, by the way, don't care if I do owe it."

Leonard ignored him, looked at the brand-new mobile home, glanced at the new tires on the truck. I saw his expression change as he turned his attention back to Thomas.

"Keep the money," Leonard said. "You might need it for buying twenty-two shells. Though I think you got a bit of money from somewhere, seeing your new home. Your old daddy, who knew you didn't like him, I'm thinking he might have given you a call to help him fulfill that fucked-up plan he had, that's what I think. You'd be all for that. Revenge and easy money in one swoop. Bet you enjoyed pulling that rope around his neck, cutting that key out of his belly, taking that money out of his bank box. It all falls into place now. Want to know what else I figure?"

"I don't give a shit," Thomas said.

"Thanks for asking," Leonard said. "My figure is you already got rid of the twenty-two you used to kill your sister and nephew. I bet you never even knew the kid's name. I know I didn't, but you should have."

"You don't know nothing," Thomas said.

"You may think you're a badass, way you could sneak up on your sister and her son, do them like you done. I got nothing for her. I think she's as big a piece of shit as you are, as Professor is. But that child never did anything to anyone. Baby's only crime far as you were concerned was it had dark skin. The kid didn't even have a personality yet."

"Get off of me," Thomas said.

"Here's something I want you to think about," Leonard said. "I want you to know that one day you'll come out of this new blood-paid mobile home on your way to pick up a six-pack, and I'll be there. Might even call your name. Surprise, motherfucker. And then it's coming. A bullet. I might even use a twenty-two, same as you. I got one, and mine can't be traced."

"I'll go to the police," he said.

"Go ahead, my word against yours. What did you hear, Hap?"

"I heard you give your condolences about his sister, nephew, and mother."

"See? That's what Hap heard. Your day is coming, cracker."

Sweat had beaded up at Thomas's hairline.

"Now, me and Hap are sorry for your loss, but we got to go. I have to oil a gun or two."

Leonard stood up. He looked at Thomas, pointed his finger at him, brought his thumb down, and said, "Bang."

57

About six months later, give or take an afternoon, I woke Brett up and asked her her favorite color and got slugged in the arm. A few minutes later I got laid, so that took the pain away.

We had breakfast together, and then she went grocery shopping.

I was sipping a cup of very fine coffee and reading our local rag, which is mostly ads these days, when something caught my eye in the police report.

BODY FOUND, the headline read.

I felt a cold chill start at the base of my spine and move up to my neck and nestle under my hairline like a solidifying glacier.

A man had been found in a ditch partially filled with water. It was a ditch down a clay road in the woods. It was surmised that the man had gone out there to dump his trash illegally.

He was found clutching a plastic bag full of beer bottles. He had a bullet hole between his eyes. A .22 caliber was suspected. Most likely shot at close range. No suspects.

Surprise, motherfucker.

The dead man's name was Thomas Mulhaney.

I took a deep breath and put the paper down on the kitchen table. I sat there and thought for a little bit. I drank my coffee. I got up and poured myself another cup, sat down again, and reread the article. It said the same thing it had said before.

I carefully folded the paper and took a sip of my coffee. It tasted bitter as reality. I got up and carried it to the sink and poured it down the drain.

From the kitchen window, I could see a crow flying south.

Joe R. Lansdale is the author of nearly four dozen novels, including *Rusty Puppy,* the Edgar Award–winning *The Bottoms, Edge of Dark Water,* and the Spur Award–winning *Paradise Sky.* He has received eleven Bram Stoker Awards, the American Mystery Award, the British Fantasy Award, and the Grinzane Cavour Prize. He lives with his family in Nacogdoches, Texas.

MULHOLLAND BOOKS

You won't be able to put down these Mulholland Books.